DEATH OF A CATTLE KING

WAYNE D. OVERHOLSER

SAGEBRUSH
Large Print Westerns

First published in Great Britain by ISIS Publishing Ltd.
First published in the United States by Five Star

Published in Large Print 2014 by ISIS Publishing Ltd.,
7 Centremead, Osney Mead, Oxford OX2 0ES
by arrangement with
Golden West Literary Agency

The moral right of the author has been asserted

CIP data is available for this title from the British Library

ISBN 978–0–7531–5353–6 (pb)

Printed and bound in Great Britain by
T. J. International Ltd., Padstow, Cornwall

DEATH OF A CATTLE KING

CHAPTER
ONE

For the Holt family this Sunday, June 16, 1878, started about the same as Sundays always started. Bruce rose later than usual, built a fire in the kitchen range, then called Mary, who was sleeping on the front-room couch. When Bruce left the house to do the chores, the sun was beginning to show above the rim-rock on the eastern side of Paradise Valley.

For once his father wouldn't grumble because they were starting the day with the sun already up, Bruce thought. Morgan Drew had spent the night with them, and hc had been responsible for the family's staying up late. In this regard, the morning was different from most Sundays, for Morgan seldom spent a night here. This time he had, probably for some devious purpose of his own. Mary had even been cheerful about giving up her bed for him, something she would not have done for anyone else.

Bruce dawdled as he fed the horses, his thoughts on a situation that was bound to come to a head in a few weeks, maybe a few days. He couldn't change Morgan Drew, who had a ruthless ambition that was cold-bloodedly brutal, but the trouble was he couldn't convince his father that Morgan had such an ambition.

Bruce was twenty-three years old, he had done a man's work here on Rainbow from the time they had started the ranch eight years ago, and not once had his father believed him when he said anything against Morgan. The truth was Sam Holt still considered Bruce a boy, while in his eyes Morgan was a mature man.

The sun was a full red circle above the rim when Bruce walked slowly across the yard to the house. Night shadows still clung to the base of the eastern rim, but they would soon be gone, for the sun was already cutting away the night chill. Another hot day, he thought absently, then his mind turned to Mary, who was in love with Morgan. He knew how Morgan was with women, but Mary simply refused to listen if he tried to tell her.

When Bruce entered the kitchen, Mary was lifting flapjacks from the hot griddle to a platter. She shoved the platter into the warming oven and dribbled spoonfuls of dough onto the griddle. She was wearing a clean, freshly starched pink dress, her blue eyes were bright with excitement, and her cheeks were cherry red. This was the way she always looked when Morgan was with her.

Morgan was washing his face when Bruce came in. He dried with the towel that hung on the wall beside the pump, nodding at Bruce and saying in his pleasant voice: "Good morning, Bruce. Short night, wasn't it?"

"Yeah, it was a short night," Bruce agreed, and pumped water into the wash pan as Morgan picked up a comb and ran it through his curly black hair.

2

He was handsome, this Morgan Drew, and Bruce would be the first to agree to it. He was twenty-nine years old, unmarried, and claimed he had never been in love before, letting Mary infer that he was now. He stood a good three inches taller than Bruce, who was an even six feet. Morgan was a typical cowman, with wide shoulders and a long-boned body that tapered down in a sort of triangle.

Morgan's small feet were encased in tight-fitting, hand-tooled boots that had cost him a small fortune in Winnemucca last fall when he and his partner, Ben Louderman, had driven the Big D herd to the shipping pens. He had probably spent more on those boots than Bruce spent on clothes in a year.

"Come to the table, Morgan," Mary said. "No use of you having to eat cold flapjacks just because Bruce and Pa can't get around."

"They sure smell good, Mary." He gave her a pat on the shoulder and she smiled at him as if she would treasure this slight caress the rest of the day. After he had sat down and Mary had placed the heaping platter of flapjacks in front of him, he added: "They look good, too, and, by golly, I know they will be."

"I hope so," Mary said, pleased. "I wouldn't want you to take that long ride to the Big D and get there with an empty stomach."

"I won't," Morgan said. "I sure won't."

Bruce's father came out of his bedroom, yawning and knuckling his eyes. He said — "Good morning, Morgan." — and crossed to the pump as Bruce sat down at the table and helped himself to the flapjacks.

3

Sam Holt was stocky in build and half a head shorter than Bruce. He and Bruce got along well on most things, but his father was a stubborn man who would not back up an inch on a subject once he had made up his mind. He had made up his mind on Morgan Drew a long time ago.

Morgan nodded at Sam and chewed and swallowed. "Good morning, Sam. You caught me with my mouth full of Mary's good flapjacks. Your wife did a fine job teaching her how to cook."

Sam stopped pumping a moment, nodded, and then finished filling the wash pan. "Yes, she did," he said wistfully. "She taught Mary a lot of things."

"I'm sure she did," Morgan said.

Morgan Drew had a way with him, Bruce told himself, a fact he would have admitted any time. His mother had died just about a year ago. She had been a wonderful wife and mother, and life had not been the same for any of them after her death.

When Sam Holt had driven his cattle and horses and two covered wagons across the Cascade Mountains and the high desert and had settled here in Paradise Valley when it was just a sage-covered bowl surrounded by rimrock, Bruce's mother had driven one of the wagons, and then had cooked over an open fire for months before the house was built. Bruce had never heard his mother complain. She had, he was sure, loved her husband and her two children with the kind of unselfish love that goes beyond human understanding.

Morgan and his partner, Louderman, and the Big D crew had come to the funeral, and so had Jason Bell, the Holts' powerful neighbor on the east side of Steens Mountain. Bruce had no fault to find with Morgan as far as the funeral went. He had visited often after the funeral, and that had been of help, but Bruce did find fault with the way he used the memory of his mother to ingratiate himself with Bruce's father and Mary. It was too much like feeding and petting a calf until he was fat, then slaughtering him.

"I hear we may have trouble with the Indians," Morgan said casually. "Old Jason Bell was telling me there's talk of the Bannocks heading this way and joining up with the Paiutes. Their chief, Buffalo Horn, was killed in a fight about a week ago. It was close to the Idaho line not far from Silver City, according to what Jason heard."

"Naw, the Paiutes won't make no trouble," Sam said. "They ain't like the Modocs, who raised so much hell a few years ago. I don't figure the Bannocks will get here, neither. They'll circle around and head back toward the reservation."

"Jason ought to know what he's talking about." Mary brought more flapjacks and sat down beside Morgan. "He's had a lot of dealings with the Paiutes."

"Yeah, he ought to know what he's talking about," Sam admitted, "but he's getting old and jumpy. I won't believe it till I see 'em coming."

Morgan winked at Mary as he sat back and reached for tobacco and paper. It was the sort of communication that often passed between them as if they shared a common knowledge about Mary's father that Bruce was too stupid to grasp. This was part of Morgan's

5

maneuvering. Somehow he had managed to convince Mary that Bruce wasn't quite bright, and she, in turn, managed to get that said in an oblique sort of way whenever Bruce tried to tell her what Morgan was up to.

Morgan sealed his cigarette and reached for a match. "I'll never forget the first time you saw the valley, Sam," he said. "Helen was driving the lead wagon and Bruce here was driving the other one. I guess Mary was in the seat with her ma, weren't you, Mary?"

"That's right where I was," she said, smiling. "You never thought then I'd grow up, did you?"

Morgan laughed. "Well, no, I guess I didn't. Not into the pretty girl that you are. All I remember was a skinny kid who was all eyes, with a ponytail hanging down her back." He turned to Sam. "What I started to say was that you 'n' me was driving the cattle. We came onto the north rim sudden-like and you just sat there in your saddle, staring down into the valley like it was a dream come true. After while you said . . . 'This is it, Helen. This is where we're going to live.'"

Sam nodded, the good memories swarming back into his mind. Bruce had started to fill his pipe, but now he cradled it in his hand, his gaze on Morgan's handsome face. His features were good, his black mustache was carefully trimmed, and his teeth, as perfectly formed as any that Bruce had ever seen, made a white streak across his bronze face when he smiled. He was the only man Bruce had ever hated in his life, hated him because he was a liar and a cheat. But still, hating him as he did, Bruce had to admit that Morgan Drew

6

possessed charm for most folks. He could turn it off and on at will, and yet he could appear sincere.

"I remember, too," Bruce said, his hand squeezing the bowl of his pipe so tightly that his knuckles were white.

Morgan glanced at him tolerantly. "You were just a kid, like Mary," he said as if Bruce had been too young to remember anything.

"I was fifteen," Bruce said. "Mary was ten."

"That's about right," Sam said. "After we got down into the valley, it was Mary's birthday, and Helen done her best to bake her a cake, but it didn't turn out real good. Purty hard to bake a birthday cake without no oven."

"I'll bet it is," Morgan agreed. "I'd clean forgot about that."

"Some of the Indians showed up that first week," Sam was saying. "They sure were a sorry-looking bunch of savages. That's why I don't believe they'll ever make any trouble. They begged for grub, but we didn't have none, so I ran 'em off with a gun. They didn't bother us none after that."

Morgan nodded. "I remember, Sam. There were ten or twelve of 'em. Took a lot of guts to do what you did, even if they was beggars."

"Oh, I dunno," Sam said, pleased. "You do what you've got to do, and after you look back on it, you wonder how you screwed up the nerve to do it."

Morgan still held his cigarette in his hand. He said: "There's something I ought to tell you, Sam, though I hate like hell to do it. I spent all day yesterday on the JB talking to old Jason. We always try to plan things out. Seeing as the Big D and the JB are the main outfits in this end of the county, I guess we just about run things." Morgan paused, turning the cigarette with his fingertips, then he went on: "It ain't quite that way, really. Ben Louderman's got as much to do with running the Big D as I have, but he usually goes along with anything I say. There's another thing, too. I don't always agree with Jason. He's a contrary old goat at times. When he gets his head set, I can't budge him. Now he's claiming he's got to the end of his rope with you. He says he's gonna make a move if you ain't out of this valley in a week."

Sam stared at Morgan, his round face turning pale. He said in a low voice: "Then he'll have to make his move."

"Hell, Sam, you can't buck a man like Jason," Morgan said as if the idea was ridiculous. "I told him I'd buy you out. I think ten thousand dollars is a fair price for Rainbow, lock, stock, and barrel."

Bruce had seen something like this coming, but he had not expected it so suddenly or for Morgan to put it so baldly. Sam should have sensed it, too, but apparently he hadn't, judging from the way he was staring at Morgan. Mary was almost as shocked.

"Morg, I wouldn't sell Rainbow for ten thousand dollars or a hundred thousand dollars," Sam said. "I thought you knew that."

"I told Jason you wouldn't want to give this place up," Morgan admitted, "but it's like I said. When Jason gets his mind set, there's not much I can do. He was

8

the first man to drive a herd of cattle into the country, you know. He had the first ranch, and right now I guess he's the biggest cattle king in Oregon, so I ain't about to buck him."

"I will," Sam said sharply. "Maybe it'll just be me 'n' Bruce against twenty JB buckaroos, but we'll buck him just the same."

"I owe you a hell of a lot," Morgan said worriedly. "That's why I'm making you the offer. I don't want to see you walk out of here without anything and I sure don't want you shot." He hesitated, his eyes on his cigarette as he turned it in his fingers. "After Pa died, you were all the father I had."

Sam acted as if he hadn't heard. The stubbornness showed in him now. It was in his gray eyes, in the thinning and lengthening of his lips. He said: "Helen's buried here, Morg. I aim to be buried beside her. I won't be bulldozed into selling out or running from Jason Bell and his bunch of tough hands."

"I just don't want to see you shot," Morgan repeated. "I don't want Mary hurt. If it comes to a fight, she can come and live on the Big D, where she'll be safe, but I was hoping to keep that from happening. I think you're being unreasonable about this, Sam. You could take the ten thousand dollars and go back to the Willamette Valley and buy a good farm."

For the first time in his life Bruce could not control his temper in front of his father and Morgan Drew. He rose and kicked his chair back against the wall.

"My God, Morgan," he said, "why don't you tell him the truth?"

He stalked out of the kitchen, slamming the screen door behind him. He heard Mary cry out: "Bruce, what's got into you?" And his father's angry bellow: "Bruce, come back here and apologize!"

But he strode on across the yard toward the corral, not looking back once.

CHAPTER
TWO

Bruce was so angry that he had trouble roping his sorrel gelding, Stony, and he took twice the time he would have normally to get the saddle on the animal and the cinch tightened. He had a date to meet Karen Bell at Skull Springs, and at the moment all he wanted was to get on the horse and ride out of the valley. His father would raise hell if he knew Bruce was meeting Karen, then he thought grimly that old Jason Bell would, too, if he knew.

Sometimes Bruce was uneasy about keeping things from his father, but he had learned a long time ago that there was less friction if he didn't talk about some of his activities. He had a feeling that this would be true when he was forty if he was still at home.

He would have to make the break sooner or later, and, after what had happened at the breakfast table, he knew it would be soon. He led Stony out of the corral and closed the gate, telling himself that as soon as this trouble with Jason Bell was settled, he'd leave home. He was convinced that the trouble was really with Morgan, not old man Bell. He'd ask Karen when he saw her.

Bruce lifted a booted foot to the stirrup, then lowered it as his father left the house, calling: "Wait a minute, Bruce!"

He waited beside the sorrel, watching his father trot across the yard to him. He had hoped to get away before he was forced into a quarrel, but now he told himself glumly that he wasn't going to be able to avoid it. One thing was sure. If his father insisted on him apologizing to Morgan, he'd do it with his fists, then he'd go into the house and pack his war bag and get to hell off Rainbow. Suddenly a perverse and reckless mood took possession of him, and he decided he'd make it plain before his father had a chance to say anything.

When his father was ten feet away, Bruce said: "If you're going to holler some more about an apology, I'll make it the minute Morg leaves the house. I'll knock hell out of him, and then I'll pull out. I've thought about it for quite a while, but I've stayed on Rainbow 'cause I figured you needed me. Now it looks like you'd best hire a good buckaroo."

Sam's mouth sagged open in sheer astonishment. This, coming on top of what Bruce had said in the kitchen, was too much. Sam swallowed and wiped a hand across his face as if not quite sure he was awake or asleep and having a nightmare.

"I reckon you don't mean that, boy," Sam said hoarsely. "I wasn't aiming to say anything more about an apology. That's between you and Morg, and, if you've got to settle it with a fight, you'll just have to do it. I reckon it's been shaping up for a long time."

12

"A long time," Bruce agreed. "Ever since his pa died and you agreed to bring him along when we left the Willamette Valley. He bullied me all that summer, but you never knew what was going on. He kept it up every chance he got till I grew up enough to handle him, then he stopped. He's a liar and a cheat, Pa. Why in hell you can't see through him is more'n I know."

He had wanted to say this for a long time and, now that he had started, the words kept rushing out of him. He saw dark anger in his father's face, saw him clench his fists at his side, saw the pulse beat in his temples, but he kept on talking.

"You think Morg's your friend and you think he'll help you in a pinch, but he won't. The trouble that's coming at us is from Morg, not Jason Bell, who's got all the range he can use. You think Morg's going to be your son-in-law, but he won't. He's got other girls in love with him just like Mary is. They think he's in love with 'em, but all he wants is to get in bed with 'em."

Sam raised a fist to hit Bruce and froze in that position as if only then realizing what he had almost done. He lowered it slowly, whispering: "What's wrong, boy, you talking about leaving home this way? This is your home and always will be. When I die, it'll go to you and Mary. Morg's got nothing to do with it. I don't know why you hate him. All I know is you're wrong about him."

"No, I'm not wrong," Bruce said. "I guess the main trouble is that Morg is the kind of son you wanted and I'm not. I'm just a boy to you. Or maybe I'm a cheap buckaroo who gets half the pay you'd have to give a stranger."

He stepped into the saddle, thinking again of that bitter day eight years ago when they'd started from the Willamette Valley with a herd of cattle bound for the Santiam Pass over the Cascade Mountains. Bruce had expected to ride a horse and help drive the cattle, but no, his father had told him to take the second wagon and follow the one his mother drove.

A few minutes later Morgan Drew had ridden up on a fine bay gelding with an expensive saddle under him and the best clothes he could buy in Albany and the fortune his father had left him in a money belt buckled around his waist. That was the way it had been all the way to Paradise Valley. Maybe it was the reason he had started to hate Morgan Drew, but there had been plenty of reasons since then, reasons that Sam Holt simply overlooked.

"Wait, Bruce." Sam took his bandanna out of his pocket and wiped his face. "I didn't know how you felt. I guess I've been sore about you hating Morgan. Seemed like it was just kid jealousy that you'd outgrow someday." He hesitated, then he said: "I reckon you're gonna be gone again today?"

Bruce cupped a hand over the horn and looked down at his father's anxious face. He'd said them at last, the words that had piled up in him through the years, and now for some reason he felt better, as if he had finally relieved the pressure that had been building up in him for so long. Then he realized there was no

14

anger in his father, that he had hurt his father by what he had said, and he was sorry.

"Yes, Pa," he said. "I'll be gone all day."

"What I came out for was to ask you to wait till Morg was ready to go," Sam said. "He told me to saddle up for him while he told Mary good bye, then he wants to ride a piece with you. Maybe it'd be best for you to go on, though, feeling the way you do."

Bruce hesitated, remembering that he had only a Winchester and Morgan was carrying a revolver, that if Morgan intended to kill him once they were out of sight of the house, he'd find it easy enough to do unless Bruce got the drop on him.

For a moment Bruce was tempted to go into the house and get his .45, then decided it would be a mistake. Morgan might regard it as an invitation to try to kill him, maybe even before they left Paradise Valley. But to ride on now would make Morgan think Bruce was afraid of him and he couldn't afford to let that happen.

"I'll wait," Bruce said.

Still Sam hesitated, wanting to say something and not knowing how to put it into words. He had never been an articulate man; he had never been one to show his emotions, either. Now he had to take a little time to sort out his words before he said: "I guess that part of the trouble was the way I felt about Morg's father. Paul Drew was my best friend. You don't remember him very well, but he owned a bank and was pretty well fixed. More than once he helped me out of some financial trouble I'd got into or I'd have lost the farm."

Sam cleared his throat and glanced at the house to see if Morgan had left yet, then he hurried on: "He had a heart attack and almost died. His wife had died two, three years before and Morg was twenty-one, but he hadn't growed up yet, not enough to take care of himself and Paul knew it. He sent for me, knowing he didn't have long to live, and he asked me to look out for Morg. A week after that Paul had another heart attack that killed him. That's why I fetched Morg along. Since then I've tried to do all I could for him 'cause he was Paul's son. I owe it to Paul the way I see it, but Morg's disappointed me a lot of times."

Suddenly tears began rolling down Sam's leathery cheeks. He whirled, took his rope from the gatepost, and went inside and caught Morgan's horse. Bruce looked at the kitchen door, wondering what Morg and Mary were doing. He thought about his father, knowing he had said too much. It had been at the wrong time, too. He should have said it a year, or maybe two years ago. He had never seen his father cry before except the day when his mother was being buried.

A moment later Sam led Morgan's big black out of the corral just as Morgan left the house and strode toward him. Bruce said in a low tone: "We'll talk again tonight."

Sam nodded, his eyes on Morgan's tall, straight-backed figure. He said: "Yeah, we'll talk tonight."

"Thanks, Sam," Morgan said when he came up.

He took the reins and stepped into the saddle. He had the air of a great lord of the manor talking to an underling who had done a small service for him. Bruce wondered if that was the kind of thing his father had in mind when he'd said Morgan had disappointed him.

Morgan lifted his Stetson to Mary, who stood on the back porch. She waved at him, then Morgan touched his horse. He swung around the corral and into the road that led to the switchback trail on the west side of the valley, one of the two breaks in the rimrock that completely surrounded Paradise Valley.

Bruce pulled in beside Morgan, glancing across the flat, fertile land that was the valley floor, all of it watered by a spring that gushed out of the ground at the base of the rim on the south side. The grass would be ready to cut shortly after the 4th of July, and for two months or more after that Bruce and his father would be working with the hay every day. Most of the Rainbow cattle were on the north shoulders of Steens Mountain. If there was any part of Rainbow that Morgan and Ben Louderman needed, it would be the mountain range. The Big D had enough meadow land.

They reached the base of the west rim and started up the twisting trail, neither saying a word. Bruce, still thinking about what was behind Morgan's latest maneuver, wondered if summer range or meadow land or anything else of that nature motivated the man. Maybe it was just his driving ambition that would not let him rest until he had consumed every ranch in the south end of Grant County and added it to the Big D. In time that would even include Jason Bell's JB.

The towering rocks on both sides of the trail hid the riders from anyone who was watching from the house or the corral. Bruce eased his Winchester out of the boot as he said: "I'm not packing an iron which same you know, Morg. If you start a fight, all I've got is my Winchester."

"You aiming to shoot me in the back?" Morgan asked.

"I wish I could," Bruce said. "The trouble is I'm not the same kind of bastard you are."

"Bragging now, ain't you?" Morgan laughed. "Well, go ahead and brag. You might not have much more time to do any bragging. I wanted you to ride a piece with me because I've got something to say I didn't want Mary or Sam to hear. I understand you've been seeing Karen Bell. Not any more. You stay away from her. I aim to marry her, and, by God, if I have to shoot you to help Karen make up her mind about me, I'll do it."

They came out on the sagebrush-covered plain, the hot, morning sun beating down on Bruce's back. They pulled up, Morgan swinging his horse around to face Bruce.

"I guess you'd try, all right," Bruce said.

"I'll get the job done, one way or another," Morgan said. "And don't let Sam forget he's got one week to sell out to me. He can walk off Rainbow with ten thousand dollars in his pocket or nothing. It's up to him."

He made no pretense of being polite now, no pretense of maintaining the charm that he wore like a coat when he was with Mary. For some reason his flushed, angry face did not seem to be as handsome as it had been in the Rainbow kitchen an hour ago.

18

Suddenly Bruce laughed. He said: "Morg, I read one time about a lizard called a chameleon that changed colors with his background. That's you all over. You were one hell of a polite fellow an hour ago when you were with Pa and Mary. Is it worth it?"

Morgan stared at him, puzzled. "What do you mean?"

"You're fixing to marry Karen Bell, which is no surprise to me, 'cause she's Jason's only kin and the JB goes with her," Bruce said, "but all the time Mary and Sue Tucker and some other girls think you're gonna marry them. You'll be in one hell of a mess if they ever get together."

"I can handle it," Morgan said, and started to ride away.

"Wait," Bruce said, and thumbed back the hammer of his rifle.

Morgan whirled his horse, shouting: "If you're aiming to kill me, give me a chance for my gun!"

"Would you?"

Morgan stared at the rifle for a moment, then raised his eyes to Bruce's face. "Sure I would."

"You're a liar," Bruce said contemptuously. "No, I ain't gonna kill you. Not now anyway. You gave me a warning. It's my turn to give you one. If you get Mary into a fix, you'll marry her. If you don't, I'll kill you."

"That all?" Morgan asked coldly.

"That's all," Bruce said.

Morgan reined around and, leaving the road that bent northward toward Camp Harney, took off through the sage toward the Big D, which lay to the southwest.

Bruce watched him for a time, noting the straight-backed, proud way he rode, and the clean, stiff-brimmed Stetson that had never been down in the dust and manure of a corral.

Bruce sighed and turned his sorrel and rode around the valley, wondering if the showdown would come at the end of the week Morgan had given Sam Holt. He glanced at the sun and shook his head, forgetting Morgan Drew. He'd be late getting to Skull Springs and Karen might not wait for him.

CHAPTER
THREE

Bruce followed the rim of Paradise Valley, Steens Mountain lifting its great bulk against the sky to the south. The higher ridges were covered with snow that would be there until late in the summer. It was this snow that gave birth to the small streams that roared down the steep slopes, then slowed when they reached the desert floor, there to be shunted into irrigation ditches and carried onto the hay meadows on both sides of the mountain and the Big D on the west. The spring that gave Paradise Valley its lush meadows very likely came from the same source, traveling underground for miles to bubble out of the ground just above the Rainbow buildings.

He rode steadily until late morning, leaving Paradise Valley behind him as he swung around small buttes and occasional peninsulas of rimrock. He kept the mountain to his right, slowly circling its northern shoulder until it was west of him.

With the sun almost noon high, he turned sharply toward the mountain and followed a narrow cañon for half a mile until he reached a small flat of grass with half a dozen cottonwoods shading the tiny trickle that flowed on down the cañon to be swallowed by the desert to the east. Just beyond the last cottonwood the wet face of the cliff made a shape that vaguely resembled a skull.

Bruce had been afraid Karen would lose her temper and not wait for him. He was at least an hour later than usual, but he was relieved when he saw her brown pony standing in the shade of one of the tall trees. A moment later he discovered Karen lying in the grass just below the spring. She was asleep, her hat tipped forward over her eyes.

He reined up and dismounted. For a moment he looked at the girl, thinking how much he loved her. Sometimes when he let himself consider the harsh reality of their situation, he felt like throwing up his hands in despair. He seldom thought about the future for that reason, forcing himself to be satisfied with the two or three hours that he had with her each week.

He knelt beside her, thinking about the miracle that had brought them together almost a year ago. Last summer Jason Bell had entertained his neighbors with horse races, neighbors being a word that was elastic enough to include people who lived one hundred miles from the JB. Bruce had been there with Stony and had won a race with him. He had intended to put Mary up on the horse for a woman's race, but she ate something at dinner that upset her stomach and she couldn't ride.

Bruce knew Karen by sight, but they had not exchanged more than ten words, so he was surprised when she came to him and offered to ride Stony. She brought him in first, beating one of her father's horses by a full length. Her father was furious, but she laughed at him and walked off with Bruce.

Perhaps that was the reason Jason Bell thoroughly disliked Bruce. When he found out that Karen and Bruce were seeing each other, he ordered Karen to have nothing more to do with him. After that it was a matter of hiding and lying and somehow tricking Jason Bell. It wasn't hard, because he was so busy with his race horses and fighting cocks and ranch business that he paid little attention to Karen, assuming that she was obeying him.

"Father was middle-aged when he married my mother," Karen said once, the only time Bruce could remember when she had been savagely bitter. "He brought her here from San Francisco. She hated the ranch and the country and, most of all, the loneliness. I think she hated herself right into the grave. Father didn't really miss her because she had never been a very good wife. Now he puts up with me and that's all. He wanted a boy, and, when Mother couldn't have any more children, she wasn't any use to him. She was just a . . . a brood mare as far as he was concerned and she turned out to be a failure."

Now, staring at the sleeping girl, Bruce told himself she deserved a better life than she'd had. Except for the housekeeper, Donna Flagg, Karen seldom saw another woman. Her father went to San Francisco every winter, where he spent most of the money he made the rest of the year, or wasted it, as Karen put it. He never took her with him. She said that sometimes she was so sick of the ranch that she didn't care whether she lived another day, that her love for Bruce was all that kept her going.

Bruce leaned forward and kissed her. She woke violently, hitting him with her small fists and rolling away from him and trying to scream. Then she realized who he was and she sat up and shook her fist at him.

"You idiot," she said. "If I had a gun, I'd shoot you. I might have choked to death. You might even have scared me to death. I tried to yell but I couldn't get my breath. Why, I've got a notion to go home and get my gun."

"Don't blame me," Bruce said. "If a man's out riding and stumbles across a beautiful sleeping woman, he's bound to be overcome by a temptation to kiss her. I was a victim of circumstances. I couldn't help myself."

She laughed. "Oh, you are an idiot," she said. "Come here. I want to be awake when I kiss you."

A moment later he admitted that there was more satisfaction in kissing a girl who was awake than a sleeping one. She said it would have served him right if she'd bitten him. After that, they sat in silence for a long time, just looking at each other.

She was a petite girl, five feet tall and weighing ninety pounds. Her eyes were brown, her hair the color of dark honey. Her lips were red and full, her nose a little on the pug side, and, because she spent most of her waking hours out of doors, her face was almost as tanned as Bruce's.

Sometimes, when he was talking to her, he would stop and just look at her as he was doing now. When she asked him what he was thinking about, he would say that beyond a doubt she was the most beautiful woman in the world. She was always embarrassed when he said that and would accuse him of being blind, but she was pleased, too. He continually marveled how wonderfully feminine she was, raised as she had been on a cattle ranch among rough men, with fat Donna Flagg her only female company.

Karen broke the spell by getting to her feet and walking to the base of the cliff. Bruce, watching her, sensed that she was more troubled than usual. She returned with a sack of sandwiches and sat down beside him.

"I'm hungry," she said. "How about you?"

"Oh, I'll be glad to eat just to keep you company," he said as if doing her a favor.

Usually she rose to the bait, but not this time. She handed him a sandwich, took one herself, then sat, staring at it. She said after a long silence: "Morgan Drew has been visiting us."

"I know," Bruce said. "He spent last night with us."

"Did he say anything about me?"

"He said he was going to marry you and told me he'd shoot me if I didn't stay away from you. I didn't suppose he knew about us."

"I told him I was going to marry you," she said. "I just got tired of fighting him off. He's important and he's rich and good-looking, so he thinks every girl is going to break her neck to marry him. I had trouble convincing him I didn't want him." She frowned. "But I didn't think he'd threaten you. I shouldn't have said it."

"Don't worry," Bruce said. "He's been threatening me in one way or another for the last eight years. I think we're coming to the end of it."

When he told her what Morgan had said about Jason Bell's giving his father one week before he made his move if Sam didn't sell out, she said sharply: "That's the biggest lie he ever told. They did have a hot argument about it. I heard most of it. Morgan wanted to tell your father what you said he did, and Father told him he was on his own if he tackled Rainbow, that the JB was as big as it was ever going to be. Then Morgan got mad and said your dad had to go, that Rainbow was the only little outfit south of the fence. Once it was out of the way, the Big D and the JB range would come together, and then Father said plain out that he thought it was a good idea for Rainbow to be between them."

"Is Jason afraid of him?" Bruce asked.

She nodded. "We all are, I guess. I don't see how your sister or Sue Tucker or any other girl could be in love with him. Even if I didn't love you, Bruce, I couldn't stand him. Under his good looks and smooth manners there's something cruel about him."

Bruce knew exactly what she meant. She had sensed it, but as a boy he had experienced it. He said: "It's queer, Karen. I don't know how to explain it, but Mary's mad at me most of the time because of the way I feel about Morgan. She thinks he's really the man he pretends to be. So does Sue, and neither one knows he's playing around with the other one, as far as I can tell. Or with you, either."

"Your father must know what he is!" she cried.

26

"He doesn't seem to," Bruce said. "Pa is a man who believes what he wants to believe and hears what he wants to hear. He's that stubborn. I guess he just wants to believe Morgan is as pleasant and courteous as he acts when he visits us."

"Your friends north of the fence know better, Verd Tucker and the rest."

"They sure do," he said. "Verd knows about Jason, too."

She stared at her hands that were folded on her lap. "I guess one's as bad as the other except that Father's satisfied with what he's got and Morgan's bound to have more."

"Does Jason still have a man riding the fence?"

She nodded. "That was something else they argued about. Father says that sooner or later the settlers will bring in a U.S. marshal and he'll order the fence taken down. Morgan said they'd face that situation when it came, that, if they didn't keep the fence up and guard it all the time, the homesteaders would move in and destroy both ranches."

"Morgan's right about that," Bruce said. "Verd has always wanted this place right where we're sitting. I suppose he'll try to move onto it someday and they'll kill him."

"Morgan would kill him, all right," she said passionately. "He's capable of killing anybody who gets in his way. Bruce, you've got to marry me. I just can't stay here on the JB any longer. We could work. Both of us. We wouldn't starve. Father's decided I'm going to marry Morgan and that's all there is to it."

"I want to get married as much as you do," he said gravely. "I used to think I could take you to Rainbow to live, but I can't now. We're going to have to fight. If it isn't with Jason, it'll be with Morg and Ben Louderman. It's bound to come as soon as the week's out, 'cause Pa won't sell."

"You can't fight an outfit as big as Morgan's," she said.

"I don't guess we'd have much chance," he admitted. "I don't know what we'll do. I'm going to see Verd and the others when I leave here. The Ninety-Nine's meeting this afternoon."

"You and your lodge or whatever you call it," she said contemptuously. "Six men. That's all you've got. It's ridiculous, Bruce. Usually you're sensible and practical, but not on this."

"I know," he said. "When you're drowning, you reach for any straw in sight, and right now the Ninety-Nine's the only straw I see."

He couldn't look at her. She was terribly right. For about a year he and Verd Tucker and four of their friends had been meeting and talking about Morgan Drew and the fence that cut off the Big D and the JB range from the northern part of the valley, a fence that illegally closed a country road that ran south to the Nevada line and blocked settlers from land that they had a right to claim.

The six of them had formed a secret organization they called the 99. They had worked up passwords and a grip and had taken an oath to preserve law and order. At first Bruce had thought they would take in other members and would operate as a group of vigilantes, strong enough to take a stand against Morgan Drew and Ben Louderman, but now he knew it had never been more than a dream.

Maybe his father was right about his being a boy. The six of them had behaved like a gang of kids forming a club in one of their backyards. The bitter truth was that no other settler in Harney Valley wanted to buck Morgan Drew or Jason Bell, and six men weren't enough. Live and let live was the motto of the other settlers. Every feeler that the six men had made to their neighbors had met with failure.

Bruce and Karen finished the sandwiches and sat holding hands, each thinking that the problem had no solution. Morgan Drew was the only one with winning cards because he had money and the power that money gave him. Harney Valley was a long way from Canon City, the county seat. The Blue Mountains formed a barrier even more important than the miles. The result was that the Grant County sheriff had little to do with this sprawling, almost empty end of the county. Besides, he was Morgan's friend. There was no use even to think about the law.

"Why?" Karen cried suddenly. "Why does Morgan have to have girls in love with him and more range and more cattle and more power than anyone else?"

"I don't think there's any why about it," Bruce said. "It's the way he is. He's like a forest fire that eats everything around it and consumes it and runs on to whatever is in front of it."

She sighed. "It was a stupid question. It's like asking why I love you or why your dad is stubborn and why Father spends so much of his time and money with race horses and fighting cocks. I guess you have to accept people the way they are."

"Or you fight 'em." Bruce thought about what would happen to Rainbow because his father refused to sell, but he didn't want Karen to worry about it, so he said: "I guess the part that puzzles me is why some people believe in Morgan and others see through him. There's nothing halfway about it. You're either his friend or his enemy."

"That's right," she said. "I told you Father was afraid of him, but that's really not true. He gets mad at Morgan for running him. He does, too, even if Father is older and maybe has more money and a bigger ranch. They argue a lot, but in the end Morgan has his way. That's why I'm afraid. If you don't take me away, they'll just wear me down."

"No, they won't," Bruce said. "I won't let 'em. Something will happen. I don't know what or when or how, but something will."

He got up and pulled her to her feet. He kissed her, wondering why he had lied to her. He didn't have the slightest hope that anything good would happen that would solve their problem. When he rode away a few minutes later, he still didn't know. If he died defending Rainbow, Morgan Drew would marry Karen. She was right about them wearing her down.

CHAPTER
FOUR

Bruce rode straight north through the sagebrush, the Blue Mountains almost lost in the haze of midday. Somewhere ahead of him a dust devil angled across the desert. The air was hot and dry, and the few clouds that drifted overhead gave no promise of rain.

He reached the gate in the fence that Jason Bell had placed here for the JB hands who were going to the fort. He had reluctantly given Sam Holt a key to the padlock, and Bruce habitually carried it because his father used the gate on Morgan Drew's end of the fence.

Bruce dismounted, unlocked the padlock, and, opening the gate, led Stony through, shut the gate, and clicked the padlock shut. He was often tempted to leave the gate open, but he would not gain anything by it. Instead, he would anger Jason Bell and likely prompt him to ask for the key back.

Mounting, Bruce rode on toward Verd Tucker's place. Verd lived with his sister Sue in a rough shack. They owned about a dozen horses, a few cows that made a poor living for them, and a garden that, with great effort on Sue's part, produced a few scrawny vegetables. They had a well and enough water for their needs, but it was hard and tasted so bad Bruce couldn't drink it.

It seemed to Bruce that Verd and Sue were stupid to live here, yet neither was a stupid person. They both had reasons, though neither seemed logical enough to make them waste their lives on a poverty spread like this.

Sue stayed because she was in love with Morgan Drew, and, if she left the valley, she would probably never see him again. Verd stayed because he had his heart set on owning Skull Springs. If Jason Bell changed his mind and permitted Verd to settle there, he would have a good small ranch with ample grass, sweet water, and protection from storms, like Rainbow, but the chance of old Jason ever giving Verd that permission was a big fat zero, and Verd knew it as well as Bruce did. Sue's chance of marrying Morgan was the same fat zero, but the difference was she didn't know it. She wouldn't believe Bruce if he told her any more than Mary would. Karen was right. You accepted people the way they were.

He reached the Tucker place half an hour after leaving the gate. It was a hardscrabble ranch that never changed from one time he was there to the next — the weathered, unpainted shack with a white spot in front of the door where Sue threw her wash water, the half dozen bedraggled hens scratching around in the dust, the privy that looked as if it would go over in the next hard wind, the slab shed with gaping holes in all four walls, and the brown haystack on the far side of the corral.

32

Four horses were tied in front of the shack. As Bruce dismounted and tied Stony beside the others, Sue left the shed, leading her saddle horse. Bruce saw her, but he started toward the front door of the shack, hoping he wouldn't have to talk to her. It wasn't that he disliked her. Actually he felt sorry for her, but he was always depressed after he was with her for even a little while.

For Sue every waking hour was filled with drudgery, and in the two years he had known her, it seemed to him that she had steadily lost hope that life would ever be any better. Not that she said it in words. She tried to be bright and cheerful, insisting that Morgan loved her and would marry her in his own good time. She was like his father in that regard, he thought, believing what she wanted to believe. Perhaps she had to believe it, perhaps this forlorn hope was all that kept her from going crazy.

Before he reached the shack, Sue called: "Oh, Bruce! I want to see you a minute!"

He turned and walked slowly toward her, thinking sourly that, if he had arrived five minutes later, she would have been gone. She moved toward him, trying to smile, but failing. When they met, he saw that her eyes were red, and he wondered if she had finally faced the truth about Morgan.

"I won't keep you more'n a minute," she said. "They're all here and Verd's getting pretty impatient. He wanted me out from underfoot, so I decided I'd go see the Daniels boys' mother. Hank said she's been right poorly."

"I guess Verd'll wait till I get there," he said.

She lowered her gaze and scraped the toe of a worn boot back and forth through the dust. She was a big woman, almost as old as Morgan. She had never even thought of being in love before, Verd had told Bruce, but Morgan's attentions had flattered her.

She had ridden away many times to keep dates with him. Where they went and what they did was a mystery to Verd because she refused to talk to him about it, but he suspected the worst. So did Bruce because Sue was the kind of woman who, if she loved a man, would do anything for him. Bruce did not condemn her because to him this was an admirable quality, but Verd did not agree.

"If he gets her into trouble, I'll kill him," Verd had told Bruce more than once.

Now, looking at her, Bruce sensed that she was deeply troubled and wondered if this was what had happened. He waited, thinking that she would be a very attractive woman if she could afford new clothes and would take time brushing and putting up her auburn hair.

"I'm worried about Verd," she said. "He's been drinking. You know what that does to him. He gets mean. The rest of them are worked up, too. They're talking pretty wild. You're the only level-headed one in the bunch. If you can't stop them, they'll all get themselves killed."

"I'll try," he said.

"How's Mary?"

"Fine."

She swallowed, glanced at him, and looked away. "Have you seen Morgan lately?"

Bruce nodded. "This morning. He stayed all night with us."

"How is he?"

"Good as ever. He put away a pile of Mary's flapjacks."

"I hope he marries her," she said. "If he does, I hope she's happy. I used to think there was something between Morgan and me, but there isn't any more. Everything he said to me was a lie. I guess that's what I really wanted to tell you."

He was surprised because he thought Sue didn't know that Morgan was chasing other women. He was certain Mary didn't know, or it would have come out in one of her angry tirades when Bruce had tried to tell her she should not get serious with Morgan.

"I suppose I'll always love him," Sue said. "That doesn't make any sense but it's not supposed to. He hasn't been here for a month, and the last time I went to see him he didn't show up where we usually meet. I finally wrote to him and he wrote back that he didn't want to see me any more. Verd says he's interested in Mary and Karen Bell. I don't blame him because they're younger and prettier than I am."

She turned to her horse and stepped into the saddle, then she said: "Tell Mary not to give him what he wants. He takes and takes, but he never gives anything back."

She rode away. Bruce, watching her, thought that life would never be the same for her. Morgan had been brutal with her, but at least he had been decent enough to cut the affair off, and that was more than Bruce would have expected.

He turned and went into the shack. All five of the other members of the 99 were there. Verd sat at the table, a half-filled whiskey bottle in front of him. The Daniels boys, Hank, who was twenty, and Pete, who was a year younger, sat on the bed. Rick Rawlins, chunky and red-faced, was twenty-five. Cole Battles, red-haired and freckle-faced, was twenty-three and the most belligerent man in the group.

Bruce said — "Howdy." — and looked around the room.

They stared at him, their faces clearly marked by their sour tempers. Verd Tucker was thirty years old and normally was level-headed and courteous. When they had gone through the rigmarole of organizing the 99, he had been elected president, partly because he was the oldest and partly because he seemed to possess some qualities of leadership. He had failed to act the leader, and Bruce had gradually come to the conclusion that electing him had been a mistake.

For a moment Bruce didn't know what to make of the sullen anger that plainly possessed all of them, but he did know the whiskey bottle had no place in this meeting. Verd had never brought one out before. Bruce took two long steps to the table, picked up the whiskey bottle, and threw it into the yard.

Verd rose, his hands fisted. "What the hell do you think you're doing?"

Bruce faced him, his chin thrust forward. "I'll tell you what I'm doing. You're supposed to be the leader of this bunch. If you've got to fill up on rotgut to do any leading, we sure elected the wrong man."

"I suppose you want the job?"

"No, I don't want it," Bruce shot back, "but I can tell you I'd do more with it than you will, tanked up on that liquid lightning. I'll tell you something else. We're like a bunch of damn' fool kids with our passwords and grips and the white caps we made and never wore. Six grown men acting like children, Verd. What the hell! I don't know what you're mad at today. I come in here and you all look at me like you want to fight. Well, I'm ready to fight, too, but not with you boys. You know what we are? We're a spit-and-talk society and nothing else."

Verd sat down, his hands opening and coming palm down on top of the table. "You're right," he said. "That's why I got the bottle out. It was the only way we could stand each other."

Bruce glanced around the room again. The sullen anger had disappeared. The others, red-faced and embarrassed, stared at the floor. He asked: "Why were you sore at me when I came in?"

"You're late," Verd said. "We've been sitting here quite a while just waiting on you. We were all set to go out and do something, but you weren't on hand to talk about it." He motioned to Pete Daniels. "Show him."

Pete was a gawky, beardless boy who looked two or three years younger than he was. He rose and stripped off his shirt, then turned so Bruce could look at his back. Bruce sucked in a long breath and swore. The boy had been whipped several days before. The long slashes, which must have bled profusely at first, had scabbed over, making long, dark streaks across his back.

"Who did it?" Bruce asked.

"Morgan Drew."

"Why?"

"I cut the damned fence," the boy answered. "We'd sold a horse to Buck Yoder in Catlow Valley and I was taking him south on the county road to deliver him to Buck. The gate was padlocked like it always is. When the guard came by, I told him what I had to do, but he laughed and said his orders from Drew was not to let anyone through. After he rode by, I cut the fence and took my horse down the road, but I hadn't gone a quarter of a mile till a couple of riders caught up with me. One of 'em held me under his gun and the other one went for Drew. When he came, they took me back to where I'd cut the fence and Drew used a blacksnake on me. I was down and I couldn't get up, so they threw me onto our side of the fence and put my horses back through the hole. Then they fixed the fence and rode off."

"I found him," Hank said as Pete put his shirt back on. "I took him home and Ma doctored him, or he'd be dead by now."

"That was Morgan Drew," Verd said fiercely. "Once it was Jason Bell's men who beat me up. We're done talking and spitting, Bruce. We're going after Drew. If that works, we'll get Bell, too."

"What do you mean, you're going after Drew?" Bruce asked.

"We're gonna wait till we grab Drew," Verd said, "and then we'll hang him. We figure that's all it'll take to bring that fence down and open up the Big D and JB range to settlement. I want Skull Springs and I aim to get it."

"No," Bruce said. "No hanging."

"So that's the way it is," Rawlins said.

Cole Battles nodded. "We figured that. Your pa fetched Drew into this country, didn't he? Your sis is sweet on him, ain't she? So we got to let him alone after him almost murdering Pete."

This was the reason they were mad, he thought. Now he felt the sullen thrust of their anger again. He looked from Verd to Cole Battles to Rick Rawlins and then to the Daniels boys, and back to Verd. They had made up their minds what they were going to do, and all the time they had been sure that he would not agree to it.

"This your idea, Verd?" Bruce asked. "What Cole said?"

"No." Verd shook his head. "I know better, but some of the boys thought that was the reason you'd buck a hanging. I didn't argue with 'em. You were late showing up and I was sore about that. I figured you're soft 'cause you ain't gone through the mill. If you'd got a beating like I did, or whipped like Pete was, you'd whistle a different tune."

Bruce shook his head. "No. I've told you, Verd. Now I'll tell the rest of you. I was in Prineville just after a lynching. Folks there said the juniper tree was bearing fruit. I seen him swinging in the wind, his face turned black, his head cocked over on one side, crazy-like. I had nightmares about it for weeks. No matter what Drew or Jason Bell has done, hanging 'em would be worse on us than on them."

"What did this feller in Prineville do?" Rawlins asked.

"Stole a horse."

"All right," Verd snapped. "So we don't hang Morgan Drew. What do you figure we'd best do?"

"Try the law again."

Verd snorted derisively. "A waste of time," he said. "I've been to Canon City three times and talked to the sheriff. I tried to get him to come to Harney Valley, but he wouldn't. I asked him to send a deputy down here. I even asked him to deputize me. He said no to all of it. I've been in Salem and I didn't get anywhere with the governor or the rest of 'em." He pounded the table. "Damn it, Bruce. They've got money and the power that money gives 'em. Just how do you figure to get a lawman to even come here and see what's going on, let alone do anything?"

"It's got to be a U.S. marshal," Bruce answered. "If we can get one of them to come to Harney Valley, they'll order that fence torn down."

They said nothing. All five sat motionlessly, glowering at him. They lived on poverty spreads, they wanted to move onto better land south of the fence, and they knew that legally they could do it. Verd was right on one thing, Bruce thought. The time for sitting and spitting was gone. The other five had reached the point where they were bound to do something, legal or otherwise. Time had built the tension, and now Pete Daniels's whipping had been the final strain.

"All right," Bruce said. "I'm asking you to wait one week. I think you owe me that. After the week's over, I've got a hunch you can get a marshal to come to Harney Valley."

He wheeled and walked out. He mounted and rode back toward the gate. He had intended to tell them about Morgan Drew's threat, but at the last minute had decided it would be a mistake. His father wouldn't want their help even if they would give it, and he was convinced they wouldn't.

Regardless of what happened to him and his father, an attack on Rainbow would be the kind of violence that could be used to induce a U.S. marshal to come to the valley. At the moment it seemed the only chance they had.

CHAPTER
FIVE

Bruce returned to Rainbow late in the afternoon. He took care of Stony, then went into the house, expecting Mary to have supper ready, but he found that she and his father had already eaten. He washed and combed his hair, feeling jumpy because of all that had happened that day.

According to Morgan, they had one week of peace on Rainbow. Then Karen had told him, if he didn't take her away, she'd be worn down to the point where she'd marry Morgan. Finally he'd found his friends angry with him because he was late. They were belligerent enough to dive headfirst into a kind of insanity that could only make the situation worse.

Mary was sitting by a front window in the living room, her sewing on her lap. The late afternoon light was so thin that she was squinting to see what she was doing. She glanced up at Bruce when he came in and looked back at her sewing again, her face flushed with quick anger.

He hesitated, realizing she had been furious with him all day because of what he had said to Morgan that morning. He should have known, but he just hadn't given it any thought. Until about a year ago he and

Mary had had a good relationship, far better than the average brother and sister, but in recent months their relationship had deteriorated. Now she was angry with him most of the time.

"How about getting me something to eat, Sis," he said as he crossed the room and placed his Winchester on the deer antlers beside the front door.

Tight-lipped, she said — "Get it yourself." — and kept on sewing.

His first reaction was a flash of quick anger. He felt like putting her across his knee and spanking her, or giving her a good shaking. Cooking was her job, not his. She had always taken care of it before, even when she was in what he called one of her "mads," but he didn't touch her or say anything. He turned and walked back into the kitchen. The coffee was still hot, and he found bread and the remains of a cold roast in the pantry.

He carried the food and a plate and silverware to the table, went back for a cup, and poured coffee into it, then sat down. His father came into the kitchen and took a chair across the table from him. He was silent as he took his pipe and tobacco from his pocket and filled the pipe.

"Don't hold it against Mary," Sam said after he'd tamped the tobacco into the bowl. "She's been upset all day. She thought Morg was going to ask her to marry him, and she blames you for him not doing it."

Bruce stared thoughtfully at his father. Sam Holt was a good rancher. He had found pleasure in working with stock and putting up hay and laying out the ditch system for the valley. Even building the house had been a source of satisfaction. Bruce had always envied him his ability to do anything and do it well, and to find enjoyment in his work.

Sam had never lacked the natural desire to get ahead, but at the same time he was not spurred by the sharp rowels of ambition the way Morgan Drew was. Bruce was certain his father would have been satisfied to live here on Rainbow the rest of his life, doing his part in running what would probably always be a two-man spread.

Perhaps because he was satisfied with his place in life, Sam was seldom upset by anything, not even bad weather or a mean horse or a cantankerous cow. But now he had the expression on his face of a man who has gone through hell. Bruce had seen that same expression the day his mother was buried, and he was reminded that tears had run down his father's cheeks that morning for the first time since the funeral.

"I reckon she thinks she's got a right to be sore at me," Bruce said slowly, "but I can tell you, Pa, Morg never has figured on marrying her. I guess you don't believe me, and I just make Mary mad when I tell her."

Sam struck a match and held the flame to the tobacco, puffing hard to get it started. He did not look up and he did not say a word.

"I saw Sue Tucker today," Bruce said. "Mary doesn't know, and maybe you don't, either, but ever since Sue and Verd settled in the valley, Morg's been carrying on with Sue. Sometimes he came to their house, mostly when Verd was gone. Now he's busted it off and Sue looks like she's been sent for and just couldn't come."

Still Sam said nothing, but sat staring at his big hands, which were tightened into fists on his lap, his pipe stem clenched between his teeth. He was like Mary, Bruce thought bitterly. He listened, but he just didn't hear.

Bruce finished his meal and pushed his plate back before Sam said: "We'd best do that talking you said we would. I've been thinking about what you said this morning. I didn't know you had thought about leaving home, though I guess I should have. Fact is, it's mighty hard to accept the fact that you're twenty-three years old and Mary's a grown woman wanting to get married."

His pipe had gone cold and he took it out of his mouth. He moistened his lips and went on. "It ain't never been easy for me to talk. It is for you. Same with your ma. I reckon that's why you two got along so well and always seemed to understand each other. Me, I just live one day after another and figure that things are gonna work out. Well, I can see now they ain't going to."

"I'm not leaving as long as there's a chance of trouble, Pa," Bruce said. "If I didn't say that this morning, I aimed to."

Sam glanced up and looked down again quickly. "Thanks," he said, "but I think you'd better. You're young. You've got your life ahead of you. It's different with me. I remember how I felt the first time I looked down into this valley all growed up in sagebrush, except that patch of green below the spring. It's like that day was yesterday. I'd seen this valley somewhere, but I'd never been here before, so it must have been in my dreams. I said to myself this is where we'll live and die. Well, it happened that way with Ma, and it's gonna happen to me. I won't budge and I won't sell to Morg, so I'll stay here and die, but there's no sense of you letting it happen to you."

"What do you want me to do, Pa?"

"That's what I've been thinking on all day," he said, staring at the pipe he cradled in his hand. "I'm going to ride to the Big D tomorrow and talk to Morg. I'll ask him plain out what his intentions are. If he don't love Mary, I'll ask him if he'll give her a job. Cooking maybe, anything to get her away from here when that damned Bell brings his bunch in and wipes me out. I can't have her here when that happens. They'll burn me out, and chances are she'll get killed before they finish me."

"Don't . . . ," Bruce began, and stopped.

No use, he told himself. Nothing would stop his father from going to Morgan, who would be glad to give Mary a job. He needed a woman, and Mary would do until he wore Karen down enough to marry her. At least that was the way Morgan would see it.

"If Morg won't or can't do anything for Mary," Sam went on, "I want you to take her to Canon City or whatever town she wants to go to. I've got about five hundred dollars saved up and you can have all of it. It'll keep both of you going until you can find work."

"Pa." Bruce leaned forward, his gaze fixed on his father's face. "Pa, you listen to me. I won't go. I'm staying here and helping you fight. We aren't licked by a hell of a lot. It'd be best to take Mary to the fort. Maybe we can hire some men to help fight. All I know for sure is that I'm staying right here. I'll live or die the same as you. This is my home, too."

"I thought you said this morning . . ."

"I know." Bruce rose and walked to the window. "I'm ashamed of some of the things I said this morning. We can work things out if we manage to hang on."

"I hoped we could talk about that, too," Sam said, suddenly eager. "If you want to stay, that is. A partnership, maybe. I've been wrong, thinking you'd work the rest of your life for what I was paying you."

"That would suit me."

Bruce thought of saying he was going to marry Karen Bell and he would bring her here, and knew at once it was not the time. Later, maybe, if they were still alive, and if his father finally got it through his head that it was Morgan Drew and Ben Louderman instead of Jason Bell who was making the trouble.

"I wanted to say one more thing about Morgan," Sam went on, "and then we'll forget him. He ain't the kind of man I wanted for my son to be. You are. I ain't ashamed of you and never have been. I want to tell you again that everything I ever did for Morg was on account of his father. I've hated myself for failing with the boy. That's why I keep telling myself I've got to believe in him."

"It ain't your fault, Pa," Bruce said. "Hell, he was a grown man when you started from the Willamette Valley with him."

"I know," Sam said. "The first fault was with his father, but the second was with me. Anyhow, I thought when we got here, he'd throw in with us. We'd have a partnership and . . . well, be just one family. I knew he had money and I didn't have much, so I figured the thing to do was to settle down here. Between us we'd build a nice house and buy some good bulls and we could have a hell of a fine outfit.

"I mentioned it to him and he just laughed in my face and said I could be satisfied with a ten-cow spread if I wanted to, but not him. When he met with Ben Louderman, he saw the possibilities of the Big D. Of course he knowed right from the first that Rainbow never could amount to much more'n it is now, so he threw in with Louderman. Since then I've tried to be friendly, partly because Mary's been in love with him ever since she was a child, and partly because I keep hoping he'll turn out to be what he pretends to be."

Sam rose and knocked out his pipe, looking at Bruce as he went on. "I still can't believe what you keep accusing Morgan of. He's proud and ambitious and all, but after being his father's best friend and doing all I have for him, he wouldn't turn on me like you claim he's going to."

"All right, Pa," Bruce said heavily.

He felt as if he kept beating his head against the side of the house. His father had come so far in his thinking and he could not go any further as far as Morgan Drew was concerned. Stupid, bull-headed, stubborn — Bruce could think of a lot of words to describe his father, but the fact remained that Sam Holt and Paul Drew had been close friends, and somehow Sam could not see Paul Drew's son in any way that was close to reality.

"Pa!" Mary screamed from the front room. "Bruce! Look!"

For a few seconds both men stood rooted there in the kitchen, staring at each other. Bruce didn't have the slightest idea what Mary wanted them to see, but there could be no mistaking the stark fear that was in her voice. Then he heard the rifle shots. Close, at least somewhere from inside the valley. There were others, too, farther away, probably from the rim.

Bruce lunged through the door and across the front room and onto the porch, his father a step behind him. He saw Karen and Donna Flagg, Jason Bell's housekeeper, riding as hard as they could toward the house, clouds of dust rolling up behind them. Karen's father and another man were fifty yards behind.

More shots. Bruce looked up at the east rim. Twenty or more Indians were lined up along the edge, some with smoking guns in their hands, others with bows and arrows. In that awful moment as he stood there, shocked by this scene that he had never imagined in his wildest nightmare, the thought pounded through Bruce's mind that Karen would never reach the safety of the house.

CHAPTER
SIX

For Bruce there was a momentary sense of weird unreality to what he was seeing that paralyzed him, then the spell was broken. He wheeled and plunged back through the front door. He grabbed his Winchester from the antlers, where he had placed it an hour or so ago, and ran back to the porch just as his father came alive and rushed into the house. Bruce took a rest on one of the porch posts, knowing he had never made a more important shot in his life.

Bullets were kicking dust up all around Jason Bell and the rider who was with him, others were reaching Karen and Donna Flagg, some even digging into the road ahead of them. The housekeeper rode as if she had been hit, but she was staying in the saddle.

Bruce lined his sights on one of the Indians and squeezed off a shot. The brave dropped his rifle and threw up his hands; he teetered on the edge of the rimrock, then plunged forward, to fall at least one hundred feet to the talus slope below.

Bruce fired again and missed, then his father was on the porch with his rifle. Just as Sam got off his first shot, Bruce tagged an Indian who had been standing beside the warrior he had killed. This one was jerked back as violently as if an invisible wire that had been attached to him had been given a sudden, powerful jerk. Sam was firing very fast without taking time to aim, but was simply spraying the rim with lead. "Get that box of shells off my bureau!" Sam yelled at Mary.

She disappeared into the house as Bruce pulled the trigger again. He was aware that the shooting from the rim had stopped, that Karen had pulled away from Donna Flagg and was almost to the house. He emptied the rifle just as his father had done. The Indians had ducked out of sight or had drawn back so they couldn't be seen from the floor of the valley. Probably they had been surprised by Bruce's accurate shooting and the spray of lead that Sam had thrown at them.

Bruce put his Winchester down just as Karen reined up in front of the house. He jumped off the porch and raised his arms to catch her as she toppled out of the saddle. A moment later Donna was there, one hand clutching her wounded shoulder, the other holding the reins.

"Give me a hand, Mary!" Sam shouted as she ran out of the house with the box of shells.

Sam reached Donna in time to catch her as she fainted. She was a big woman, and, as limp as she was, she was difficult to carry. Sam and Mary took her inside, and, when Jason Bell and the second man reached the house, Bruce was still holding Karen's trembling body in his arms.

The second man was Long Tom Harper, a buckaroo who had come north from California years ago with Jason Bell when he had driven his first herd into the country and had started the JB. He was Karen's favorite among her father's hands, and had often told Bruce that, if she ever owned the JB, she would make Harper her foreman.

Harper dismounted and shook his fist at the east rim, his other hand resting on the shoulder of his trembling, sweat-gummed horse. "By damn, that was close," he said. "Jason and me stood 'em off just before the women started down the trail. Them devils jumped us 'bout half an hour after we left the JB and ran us all the way to the rim. They was gaining on us, so we pulled up and threw a little lead at 'em. That discouraged 'em for a while, but by the time we got to the bottom, they was on the rim. Seemed like bullets and arrows was filling the air all around us."

Harper said all of this in the hope that Jason Bell would cool off, Bruce thought. The old man was still in the saddle, his heaving horse standing, spraddle-legged. He was a big man with long white hair and a drooping mustache and square-cut beard as white as his hair. In spite of his age, he was an active man who could go on roundup and put in a day's work as well as Harper or any of the other buckaroos. Now he leaned in his saddle, his bright blue eyes filled with antagonism. "Better get down and we'll take care of your horse, Mister Bell," Bruce said.

"Yeah, you just about rode old Nero to death," Harper said. "Better let us work on him a little."

"I'll take care of him," Bell said stiffly as he swung down. "But before I do, Holt, I want an explanation of

52

why you're standing there with your arms around my daughter."

Jason Bell was an imperious, dictatorial man, proud of his wealth and power and accomplishments. Over the years he'd had nothing more to do with Sam Holt and Rainbow than he'd had to; he made it plain that he considered himself better than Sam or the small ranchers north of the fence.

This attitude, Bruce suspected, was the basic reason he welcomed Morgan Drew and made a point of getting along with him. He had little respect for Ben Louderman, who was a tiny, bowlegged man who knew the cattle business but lacked the great pride and driving ambition that was so much a part of both Jason Bell and Morgan Drew.

Now, to have this man challenge him in a rude and hostile tone of voice was too much. It was certainly more than Bruce had any intention of taking. Karen had been almost hysterical when she'd arrived, but she was calm now. "We might as well have it out," Karen whispered. "I'll talk to him."

"No," Bruce said in a low tone. "This is my job and I'm going to do it right." He stepped away from Karen and moved toward her father. "Mister Bell, we just saved your life, and probably the lives of Harper and your daughter and your housekeeper."

Bruce stopped, his gaze not wavering from Bell's bearded face. The old man tried to outstare him, tried simply to roll over him as he did everyone who had the temerity to stand against him, but in the end he was the one who looked away, his Adam's apple bobbing up and down in his throat.

"I will admit that," Bell said. "We wouldn't have stopped here if it hadn't been a matter of life and death. We hoped to get to the fort, but they was outrunning us and we saw we couldn't make it. This was the only chance we had." He swallowed, his Adam's apple bobbing up and down in his throat again. Then he added: "I don't want to appear ungrateful."

His father would have something to say when his time came, Bruce thought. It was a strange fate that had brought Jason Bell to Rainbow needing help, with Sam Holt believing the old man had given him a week to sell out to Morgan Drew. Fate or luck or whatever he wanted to call it, Bruce saw that this was the best opportunity he would ever have to drive a bargain with Jason Bell.

"It strikes me that's exactly what you are being," Bruce said. "You want an explanation of why I'm standing with my arm around your daughter. All right, I'll give it to you. She was pretty hysterical when she got here and I think she would have fallen out of her saddle if I hadn't caught her."

"All right," Bell said stiffly. "Tom, take our horses to the corral and walk 'em. I think Holt will be willing to look after Karen's and Donna's horses. We'll need them to ride to the fort in the morning."

"You sure will if you keep riding your high horse because you won't be welcome on Rainbow," Bruce said hotly.

The old rancher's attitude galled him to the point where he didn't care what he said or how he said it. For once Jason Bell owed something to someone else.

As Harper led the horses away, Karen stepped forward to stand beside Bruce. She started to say something, but her father, outraged by Bruce's tone and words, bellowed: "By God, if you think I'm going to get down on my knees to you, you're loco! I'll get back on my horse and ride to the fort tonight before I'll do that to any man. I told you I knew you'd saved my life and I didn't aim to appear ungrateful."

"Father, we want to tell you . . . ," Karen began.

"No, I told you I'd handle this and I'm going to," Bruce said, "but your father hasn't ever had to eat even a spoonful of crow since he came to Oregon. He's going to today. You see, Karen and I love each other, and we're going to get married."

Jason Bell looked as if he were about to have a stroke. His face turned dark red; he stared at Karen, then at Bruce, and finally his gaze returned to Karen. He moistened his lips, and suddenly he began to tremble.

"Karen," Bell said in a low tone, "I told you a long time ago that you were not to see this man again. Have you disobeyed me?"

"Yes, that's exactly what I've done," she said. "I've seen Bruce almost every Sunday. The only Sundays we haven't seen each other was when the weather was so bad we had to stay home. You haven't cared what I did or who I saw or even what happened to me. You've been so busy with your real interests you haven't bothered with me."

"We'd like your approval," Bruce said, "but if we don't have it, we'll get married anyhow."

"You ain't marrying him!" Bell shouted, his anger boiling up close to the point where he would lose control of himself. "I made it clear to you yesterday when Drew was on the JB. You're marrying him."

"I'm eighteen," Karen said. "You can't force me to marry anyone."

"And you can't keep us from getting married," Bruce added.

"Karen, get back on your horse!" Bell was in a towering rage, and, when he turned to yell at Harper, his voice was high-pitched and trembling: "Tom, put them saddles back! We're heading for the fort right now!"

"I'm not," Karen said, "and Donna isn't able to ride."

Harper had stripped gear from both horses. Dumbfounded, he stared at Bell, then he called: "Jason, I reckon you can commit suicide if you want to, but I ain't hankering to let them red devils take my hair! If you try it, you'll be on foot. These horses ain't going any farther today."

"We don't have any horses to loan you," Bruce said.

Bruce knew it was brutal and wicked, and probably it was the first time in years that Jason Bell had been in a position where he could not cope with the situation that faced him. In this moment he was stripped of his

56

wealth and power; he did not even have the respect of his own daughter.

Sam left the house and came toward them. Glancing at him, Bruce sensed that his father was trapped in a position where he, too, was almost helpless. He had every reason to hate and despise Jason Bell, but he was a man who felt his responsibility as a host, and he would not under any circumstances ask or even permit Bell to leave Paradise Valley with certain death facing him if he did.

"Your housekeeper's got a bullet hole in her shoulder," Sam said stiffly. "We've put her to bed. My daughter's with her. It ain't dangerous but it's hurting her."

"We'd better see about her," Karen said.

She walked into the house, her shoulders back, her trim breasts thrust forward in the self-possessed, confident way she had when she felt her rights must be defended. Looking at her as she moved toward the house, Bruce felt a great glow of pride. The only other occasion when he had seen her walk this way had been the day of the races when she had come to him and offered to ride Stony.

"You'll never make her marry Morgan," Bruce said. "There's too much of you in her."

Bell looked at Bruce, and then at Karen's back, and at Bruce again. Suddenly and unexpectedly he grinned. "You're right," he said. "I should have known." He followed her into the house.

Sam took the reins of Donna Flagg's horse and started toward the corral. Bruce, leading Karen's horse,

57

caught up with him. Bruce said: "You might as well know, too, Pa. Karen and I are in love and we're going to get married. Nobody can stop us, not even Jason Bell."

Sam glanced at him, then looked at the corral ahead of them. "She's a pretty girl and she's got spunk. Bell ain't spoiled her, judging by the way she stood up to him. I guess you're good enough for her in spite of anything he thinks."

"I'm satisfied if Karen thinks I'm good enough for her," Bruce said.

This was a sad day for Jason Bell, Bruce thought, a day when his pride and dignity had been taken from him. In time it might prove to be a sad day for Morgan Drew as well.

CHAPTER
SEVEN

When Bruce returned to the house with his father and Long Tom Harper, Mary had a meal ready. Harper washed and sat down at the table with Jason Bell and Karen, who had been in the bedroom with Donna Flagg.

"How is she?" Bruce asked.

"She hurts," Karen said. "It's just a flesh wound, but she lost some blood, and of course her shoulder gives her a lot of misery, but the trouble mostly is that she's scared. She's afraid the Indians will attack the house, and she keeps asking when we're going to start for the fort."

"We'll go in the morning," Jason said. "Sooner or later they'll attack the house, so I figure none of us will be safe till we get to the fort."

"She needs a doctor," Karen said fretfully. "That worries her, too. We stopped the bleeding with some cobwebs, but she might get blood poisoning."

"She'll have a doctor by this time tomorrow," Jason said. "You tell her that."

"It won't be much comfort," Karen said, smiling a little. "You see, she wants to go to the fort, but she's afraid she can't get there because she can't ride a horse."

"We'll put her in my wagon," Sam said.

"Even that isn't going to make her feel better." Karen picked up her coffee cup and took a drink, then set it down. "She's got the idea she's going to die. She says that if we go to the fort, the Indians will pick us off between here and there. I can't say anything that makes her feel different, seems like."

"It's a lot of hogwash." Jason snorted. "We'll have four men instead of two. They won't have the guts to tackle us. If they do, we've got twice as many guns to fight 'em off."

"Just one thing, Jason," Harper said. "We might as well face facts. I figure we'll be safer if we stay right here. You know there ain't more'n a handful of men at the fort. The Indians could take it in half an hour if they wanted to."

No one said anything for a time. Sam had pulled a chair up to the table and had seated himself across from Jason Bell. Now he took pipe and tobacco from his pocket and filled the pipe, scowling as he tamped the tobacco down. Bruce, vaguely uneasy after thinking about what Harper had said, walked across the front room to the door and stood listening, his gaze raking the southern rim, which made a straight, black line across a lighter sky.

The sun was down and within a few minutes the twilight would become night. He remembered that only a few hours before he had sat holding Karen's hand at Skull Springs and telling her that something would happen. Well, it had happened, all right, but he wasn't sure they were any better off because of it. They would be as dead if they were killed by the Paiutes as they would be if they were shot by Morgan Drew and his cowhands.

He returned to the kitchen. No one had said anything in the time he had been gone. Gloom had settled down upon all of them like a black fog, and Bruce had the feeling they'd lost hope and were considering themselves dead right now. Even haughty, imperious Jason Bell looked as if he did not expect ever to give another order.

Bruce knew he couldn't let the situation stand this way, so he said sharply: "It isn't that bad. We've got to go to the fort because Donna needs a doctor. We'll put guards out tonight. Pa and I will take the first shift till midnight. Mister Bell, you and Long Tom will take it from midnight till dawn. We'll have an early breakfast and get rolling as soon as we can."

Karen looked at him, a quick smile tugging at the corners of her mouth. "That's more like it. For a little while there I thought you were going to say we'd save the last bullet for ourselves. Isn't that what we're supposed to do to keep from falling into the hands of savage Indians?"

"Are you trying to joke about this?" Mary demanded. "I don't think it's the least bit funny. I'd rather kill myself than let those . . . those dirty Paiutes have me."

"Quit it," Bruce said. "They aren't going to get you. I'll take a long look from the rim before we start. It's

61

only about twenty miles to the fort. We won't have any trouble."

"But if there's only a handful of soldiers at the fort," Mary said, "I don't see that we'll be any better off than if we stay right here." She turned to Harper. "How many are there?"

"The last time I was at the fort they were down to thirteen men," Harper said. "That's hardly more than a caretaker detail. A couple of friendly Paiutes came to the JB this morning to warn us. We've all heard about the fight between the volunteers and the Bannocks somewhere around Silver City and we know Buffalo Horn got killed. What we didn't know was that the Bannocks are here and they've talked Egan . . . he's the Paiute war chief . . . into leading 'em. That's why we lit out for the fort. Them friendlies didn't know how many Paiutes would fight, but they said most of 'em would. They figured we didn't have more'n a few hours and they sure was right."

"The Paiutes ain't fighters," Sam said testily. "I dunno 'bout this. Bruce, it strikes me we'd do better staying here."

"No," Jason Bell said. "Your boy made a lot of sense. I know Egan. He's a fighting man and don't you ever doubt it. The Paiutes are willing to listen to the Bannocks, most of 'em anyhow, because they've been getting madder and madder over some things that have been happening to 'em on the reservation."

"Yeah, we should have seen this coming," Harper said. "The last few days several big bands of Paiutes have rode past the JB toward the mountain. There's a passel of 'em, too, enough to wipe us out and take the fort to boot. The thing is I don't think they will. They're gonna head north and try to meet up with the Umatillas. Some even say Egan was born a Umatilla."

"They won't tackle the fort," Bruce said. "A lot of us will be pulling in there, enough men to fight off the Paiutes and the Bannocks, too. Where's your crew, Mister Bell?"

"I dunno," Jason answered. "They were south of the ranch about ten, twelve miles the last I heard from McQueen. They may have had a scrap with the Indians before now."

McQueen was the JB foreman, a good man, Bruce thought, who would bring his men through if anyone could. Bruce said: "They'll be riding into the fort tomorrow sometime. Morgan and Louderman will be along with their crew. I can think of a dozen more. We'll have fifty men there. Besides, the soldiers will be along in a few days. The Army can't let an outbreak like this go on."

"It doesn't sound so bad, does it, Mary?" Karen asked.

"No, I guess not," Mary answered as if only half-convinced.

Karen rose. "I'll go look at Donna, then I'll come back and help with the dishes."

"Wait." Sam took his pipe out of his mouth and motioned at Karen with it. "I've got something to say to your pa before you go, something that concerns all of us."

"Let it go for now," Bruce said.

"No, I ain't gonna let it go," Sam said. "I don't propose to run these folks off, but I've been damned mad ever since Morgan rode off this morning. A little sick, too. I aim to have it out right now."

Karen walked around the table and laid a hand on Sam's shoulder. "Bruce told me about it today, Mister Holt. It was Morgan talking, not my father. Please believe that. We can't afford a quarrel. Bruce is right. We've got to work together. It's the only chance we have against the Indians."

"What the hell are you talking about?" Jason demanded. "If this has got anything to do with Karen marrying . . ."

"No!" Sam snapped. "It's got nothing to do with Karen. Morgan stayed here last night. He had been with you on the JB, he said. He told me I had to sell out to him. He did offer me a fair price. I've got no complaint on that. It's just that this is my home and I don't aim to sell to him or nobody else. If I have to fight you and your whole crew, I'll do it."

"Fight me?" Jason shouted incredulously. "You must have been eating locoweed. Why should you fight me? My God, man, it isn't any concern of mine. It's between you and Morgan Drew."

"He said it was between you 'n' me," Sam shot back. "He said you'd got to the end of your rope with me and I had one week to sell out to him or you'd make your move."

"Move? Why, he's a damn' liar. If I live through this Indian ruckus, any move I make will be in a hay meadow. We'll start haying in a few days." Jason shook

64

his head as if he could not make any sense out of this. "I don't aim to bother you if you don't bother me, and you never have."

"Morgan talked to you about it, Father," Karen said. "Remember?"

"Hell yes, I remember!" Jason snapped. "I told him that if he pushed you off your range, he was doing the job by himself. I've got all the grass I need and all I want. I'm an old man, Holt. I don't want anything more'n what I've got." He rose, sour-tempered, and jerked his head at Harper. "Come on, Tom. Let's get a little sleep before midnight."

Sam sat motionlessly, watching the two men leave the room and go out through the front door. He looked at Bruce as he said grimly: "One of 'em is a liar. If Morg shows up at the fort, I'm going to find out which one it is."

For a time the silence in the room was so oppressive that it seemed unbearable to Bruce. His father thought Jason Bell was the liar. What would he do when he faced both Jason and Morgan? What would Morgan do? He would not want to lose Jason's friendship, so he could not deny that he had lied.

Bruce said: "You girls stay inside the house." He turned to his father. "I'll take the corral and shed, Pa. You watch the house."

He left the kitchen, picked up his rifle, and walked out of the house into the darkness. A great weight seemed to press against his chest so hard that it was difficult to breathe. As he crossed the dust-covered yard to the corral, he wondered if life would ever be simple enough for him to have nothing to worry about except the price of beef.

CHAPTER
EIGHT

The night turned cool as it usually did after the sun had gone down. Bruce walked briskly around the corral to keep warm, stopping often to listen for sounds that did not belong to the night, but he did not hear any. A slight wind, heavy with the scent of sage and dust, breathed in over the western rim. Overhead the stars came out, sparkling with a brilliance that Bruce had never seen when he lived in the Willamette Valley.

There was no moon, and Bruce regretted that because the darkness gave the Indians a chance to reach the corral without being seen. He felt reasonably sure the corral would be their target because they would be after horses. If the rumor was true about Egan's leading the combined Bannock-Paiute bands north to join up with the Umatillas, they would have an urgent reason to steal all the horses they could.

Once Bruce's father crossed to him from the house, asking: "Hear anything?"

"Some coyotes from the rim. That's all."

"Sure they were coyotes?"

"I think so," Bruce answered. "I don't figure even an Indian could come that close to sounding like the real thing."

"I don't have no respect for the Paiutes," Sam said, "but the Bannocks might be different. I heard a feller talking at the fort one time about the Bannocks. He claimed they sounded more like a coyote than a coyote could."

Bruce laughed. "Sometimes I think the Indians get more credit than they've got coming."

"I know the Paiutes do," Sam agreed. "Well, keep your eyes peeled."

Bruce resumed his pacing, wondering if his father was scared. Bruce knew he was, but his fear was not the paralyzing kind that comes on occasion to a man suddenly and unexpectedly. He had felt that way once tonight when he'd heard Mary scream and he'd run out of the house to see Karen and Donna Flagg riding toward him, the Indians' bullets kicking up dust all around them. He knew that actually he had not stood motionlessly for more than a second or two, but time was always relative and it had seemed to him he'd stood there frozen for minutes.

This was a different feeling, a strange tightening of his stomach muscles, a tension that made him question every sound that came out of the night. So, near midnight, when he heard running steps between the house and the corral, his heart began to pound as if threatening to jump out of his throat. He started toward the house, then stopped, not knowing what to expect because the steps were too light and fast to be his father's. It had to be one of the girls, although he had told them to stay inside.

A moment later a small, vague shape appeared in front of him and he heard Karen's voice. "Bruce."

"Here." He was both relieved and irritated, and he could not keep anger out of his voice when he added: "What are you doing? I told you . . ."

"I know what you told us, honey," Karen whispered. She put her hands on his arms, her face a pale oval in the darkness, her features indistinct. "Please don't get mad at me. I just wanted to be kissed before I went to sleep."

"Oh, for . . ." He stopped, biting back the hot words that almost tumbled out before he could control them. "Indians all around us scheming how to steal our horses and kill us and maybe sneaking up on us right now, and you want to be kissed."

"That's right," she said amiably. "Now why don't you oblige?"

He kissed her, a half-hearted effort because he was listening, thinking that at this very instant a half dozen Paiute warriors might be crawling toward the corral gate. He pushed her away, saying: "You get back to the house *pronto*."

"What's going to happen, Bruce?" she asked in a low tone. "I mean, when we get to the fort and your father sees Morgan and asks him about what Father said?"

"I don't know, but we'd better be ready for an explosion." He gave her a push toward the house. "Now will you please . . ."

"Just one more thing, honey," she said. "This is really what I came out for. I've been talking to Mary. I told her Morgan had done everything he could to make me marry him and had even talked Father into ordering me to marry him. She called me a liar and said I was just jealous and that Morgan was going to marry her in a few days."

He had been afraid this would happen. He said with more bitterness than he intended: "Haven't we got enough trouble without you and Mary fighting?"

"Oh, we aren't fighting," Karen said. "It's just that I feel sorry for her. I really do. I feel sorry for any girl who's in love with Morgan Drew. I wouldn't have told her except that I thought it might help her get over feeling the way she does, but she wouldn't listen. Well, I'm tired of his lying to us. When we get to the fort, I'll face him in front of Mary just like your father's going to."

At any other time the prospect of two girls facing Morgan Drew and asking him which one he really intended to marry and watching him try to squirm out of an embarrassing situation would have made him laugh, but not now. He said: "All right, you and Mary do that. Now you get back into the house."

"All right, too," she said tartly. "I'm sorry I bothered you."

She whirled and ran toward the house. He stood motionlessly, staring into the darkness until he could not see her or hear her steps, then turned toward the corral gate. The next instant dark figures materialized out of the darkness and rushed toward the gate. "Indians!" Bruce yelled, and fired at the one nearest to him.

70

He ran toward the corral gate, firing again but not sure he had hit his target. The important thing was to keep the Indians from opening the gate. He was panicky when he realized how helpless he and his father and the rest would be if they lost their horses.

He glimpsed the shadowy figure of a warrior in front of him and swung his rifle like a club, cracking the head of the Indian. Another one appeared out of the darkness and lunged at him, a knife slashing at him. He ducked and dived for the Indian's legs as his father fired from somewhere behind him.

Bruce brought the warrior down, the swinging knife missing him again. He drove a knee into the brave's crotch and heard a yelp of pain. Again the knife struck at Bruce; he felt a sharp, stinging pain along his ribs, but he didn't think he was badly hurt.

For a moment there was a crazy hauling and pulling and tugging, Bruce afraid that the Indian would get him again with the knife, but he caught the brave by the throat, his thumbs squeezing the windpipe. He kept his grip in spite of the bucking and twisting of the sinewy body under him. Sometime during the rolling and tumbling the Indian lost his knife. After that all he could do was to beat at Bruce with his fists, futile blows that failed to break the grip on his throat. Then, suddenly, he went limp, his arms falling to the ground.

Bruce got up, felt along the ground for his rifle, and found it, just as Jason Bell and Long Tom Harper ran out of the shed. In the darkness they were unable to see who to shoot at or even to determine what was going on. Sam Holt had clubbed one Indian to the ground.

The rest had fled. A moment later Bruce heard the hoof beats of several horses racing toward the trail to the west rim.

"You all right, Pa?" Bruce called.

"Sure, I'm all right," Sam answered. "How about you?"

"I feel like I lost some hide along my ribs," Bruce said.

"Get into the house and have the girls patch you up," Sam said. "We won't have no more trouble. The dirty boogers ran into more of a hornet's nest than they figured on."

"Must have been some bucks who knew where the gate was," Jason Bell said as he walked toward the corral from the shed. "They were after the horses, weren't they?"

"That's what they were after, all right," Sam said. "Go on, Bruce. We'll look around and see how many we got."

Bruce walked to the house, thinking that Jason was probably right that the raid had been made by some young Paiutes who had visited here and knew exactly where the gate was. They probably thought that a quick attack would free the horses, and they'd have the animals out of the corral before the whites recovered from the surprise.

By the time Bruce reached the front door, he was so angry at Karen that he was determined to tell her she had almost got them both killed. But as he stepped through the front door, a match flared and Mary

72

lighted a lamp. Karen, standing in the middle of the room, was crying.

"Don't say it, Bruce," she sobbed. "Don't say it. I know you were right. I should have stayed in the house. I almost got you killed. I'm sorry. That's all I can say. I'm just sorry."

There was no need to tell her anything. He said: "Maybe you can patch me up. One of 'em scraped a little hide off my ribs."

"I'll get the whiskey bottle and some clean cloth," Mary said before Karen could volunteer. She waited a moment, staring at Karen and letting her know how much she hated her, then walked into the kitchen.

Karen wiped her eyes. "Oh, I don't know what's the matter with me. I've done just about everything wrong. I didn't think the Indians would come down into the valley tonight. Not even to steal the horses."

"Well, they did and we're still alive," Bruce said. "Don't worry about it. Or about Mary, either. She's been mad at me for months."

He stripped off his shirt and laid down on the couch. Mary returned with long strips of cloth for a bandage and a bottle of whiskey. She examined the wound, then dribbled whiskey over it, and wrapped his body with a tight bandage.

"It isn't deep," she said, "but it'll sting some, looks like. It isn't bleeding much, either."

"Yeah, it's stinging," he said as he sat up and put his shirt back on.

It stung enough to keep him awake until dawn. He lay in the shed beside his father, who had dropped off to sleep at once. He thought about Morgan Drew and what might happen at the fort. At least both Mary and his father would see behind the mask that Morgan had worn so carefully when he had been with them, and that, he told himself, would be one good thing that would come out of all this trouble.

CHAPTER
NINE

When the first pale light of dawn began showing above the eastern rim, Long Tom Harper opened the shed door and called that it was time to get up. Bruce woke his father and went outside and washed in the horse trough. Three Indians had been killed in the attempt to steal the horses, but Bruce did not see the bodies.

"No more trouble?" Bruce asked.

"Nary a sign," Harper answered. "I heard some coyotes yapping from the rim and it sounded to me like one or two was fakes, but I wasn't sure. I dragged the carcasses of the dead Injuns around to the other side of the shed so I wouldn't be stepping on 'em. Jason, he's yonder by the house. I guess he didn't have no trouble, either."

Sam came out of the shed, yawning and scratching. He grumbled: "That was a hell of a short night."

"It may be a long day," Bruce said. He passed Jason on his way to the house, pausing long enough to say: "Looks like they didn't want no more."

"They sure didn't," Jason agreed. "I'll bet the rest of that wolf pack is halfway to the Columbia by now."

Bruce went on, thinking that Jason was more optimistic than he had any right to be. If they reached the fort today without seeing any Indians, Bruce would be surprised, but he saw no point in saying so. He built a fire, then woke Mary, who got up at once and started breakfast.

"Maybe you ought to get Karen up," Bruce said.

Mary whirled on him. "If you want her up, you get her up."

He looked at the angry girl, feeling sorry for her. In time she would be another Sue Tucker, disappointed, without hope, letting her hair and clothes go and perhaps not even caring whether she lived or died. There was a quality about Morgan Drew that Bruce did not understand, a quality that generated a passionate hatred for him or fanatical loyalty, perhaps even affection.

"All right, I'll get her up," Bruce said after a long moment of silence, Mary standing there and glaring at him as if she were inviting a quarrel. "I wish you didn't feel this way about her. She's going to be your sister-in-law."

"She'll never marry you," Mary said as if the very thought were ridiculous. "She's Jason Bell's daughter. You forget that?"

"No, but Jason won't keep her from marrying me."

Mary laughed scornfully. "Well, you ought to hear what she says about Morgan. It's worse than the lies you tell."

Bruce walked away, resolved never to quarrel with Mary again, and never to say a word against Morgan to her. If she were to understand the kind of man he was, she would have to learn in the same tragic way Sue Tucker had.

Karen had slept with Donna Flagg in Sam's room. Bruce tapped on the door and called: "Time to get up."

"I'm awake," she said.

He went outside to join his father and Jason Bell and Long Tom Harper, the three of them standing beside the horse trough and studying the rim around the valley in the thin light. They were uneasy and jumpy, and Bruce told himself this was indeed going to be a long day.

"Mary's getting breakfast," Bruce said, "but I thought we'd better water and feed the horses. As soon as we eat, we'll saddle up. While I'm riding to the rim, you can harness the team and move Donna into the wagon. If I don't see any sign of 'em, you start up the trail."

"You're sure you can get a wagon out of this hole?" Jason asked doubtfully. "That trail we came down yesterday ain't a wagon road by a damn' sight."

"The road goes out the west side," Bruce said. "It isn't a real good road, but we've been taking wagons up and down it for eight years."

Jason grunted something as if he didn't believe it and started toward the corral. By the time the men were done with the horses, Mary had called breakfast.

Karen was in the kitchen trying to help, and Mary was trying even harder to keep her from it. Bruce went to Karen and kissed her, and with his mouth close to her right ear, he whispered: "Come and sit down."

She nodded, her lips pressed together in a tight, angry line. Bruce asked: "How's Donna?"

"Sick," Karen said. "The wound's awfully red and I'm afraid she's running a fever."

"We'll have a doctor for her by dark," Bruce said. "Pa, we may be stuck in the fort quite a while. We'd better pack up enough grub to last us several days and put it in the wagon."

Sam nodded. "I was thinking that, too. I sure don't want to buy nothing at the fort I don't have to."

As soon as they finished eating, Bruce rose and stepped into Sam's room for the glasses. He paused at the bed, asking: "How do you feel, Donna?"

"I don't feel good," she said. "Karen told me you were wounded in the fight last night."

"It isn't bad," he said. "I just lost a little hide. Hurts some, though."

He picked up the glasses from the top of the bureau, took a box of rifle cartridges from the top drawer, and left the room. The woman was feverish, all right. They didn't have any time to lose. He wasn't even sure a doctor could save her, supposing they could get one to risk his own life out here. Just being in the fort might do her more good than a doctor. She was panicky with fear, and the fear would be in her until they reached the fort.

Jason and Harper left the house with him. As soon as he finished saddling Stony, he said: "Better keep things moving. Put Donna in the wagon and take her to the base of the rim. By then I'll have had time to look around. I'll wave my hat if it seems all clear."

78

Jason nodded. "We'll have her there." He paused, scowling, and then said angrily: "I may be burned out before I get back. I came to this country to raise cows, not to fight Indians. I never thought this would happen."

Bruce mounted and rode away, thinking that none of the whites in Harney Valley had expected an Indian war. Many of the Paiute bands had drifted back and forth between Oregon and Nevada, and some had wandered into northern California.

They had always been peaceful. A few of the men had worked on the cattle ranches, and several of the bands had drawn supplies at the Malheur reservation. The truth was that most of the whites had looked down on the Paiutes, considering them indolent and ignorant and dirty, and now the thought struck Bruce that perhaps this attitude was one thing that had triggered the uprising.

He had to pull Stony down on the steep grade out of the valley. By the time he reached the rim and could look back, he saw that Jason and Harper were carrying Donna from the house to the wagon. Bruce reined up and looked around. He saw nothing that moved except a couple of jack rabbits, leaping away through the sage, and several antelope far to the west.

The sun was well up and beginning to cut away the night chill. He put the glasses to his eyes and carefully studied the country around him. Still, he saw nothing to alarm him. A coyote slinking through the grass, another jack rabbit, a hawk overhead that made a slow, wheeling turn — that was all. He leaned over the rim and waved his hat. Harper was driving the wagon. When he saw Bruce, he waved back and started up the grade. Sam was directly behind him on his horse, Mary and Karen following him, with Jason bringing up the rear.

Again Bruce swept the sea of sage and grass with his glasses, then took more time to study the north shoulder of Steens Mountain. He had a strong feeling that this first hour would be decisive. If the Indians had started their race to the Columbia to join the Umatillas, they might be miles west of here by now, but if they were still gathering horses and preparing for their flight, they could be anywhere. Because of the attempted raid last night, Bruce thought this was more likely the case.

Northward the floor of Harney Valley seemed level, but Bruce knew better. He had been to Camp Harney many times, and he was very much aware that there were a number of ravines between here and the fort that were deep enough to hide a large band of Paiutes. There was nothing to do except move as fast as they could toward the fort and hope that none of the ravines held a band of raiders.

For Bruce, waiting alone on the rim, the climb to the top took a long time. Stony, sensing Bruce's nervousness, jittered around as if he, too, thought it was taking far too long to get the wagon to the top. When it finally rolled out onto the flat, Harper wiped his forehead and shook his head at Bruce as if to say he wouldn't live in that hole for all the steers in Harney County.

Bruce motioned to the north and Harper nodded and drove past Bruce, who waited for his father. When Sam reached him, Bruce said: "Why don't you go on and open the gate, Pa?" Sam nodded and galloped by the wagon. Bruce fell in beside Karen, saying: "The ride's going to be hard on Donna."

"I know," Karen said, "but we did the best we could for her. She's on a feather bed. Anyhow, I think she'll feel better just getting started."

Bruce nodded, thinking that was true. Ten minutes later they rode through Morgan Drew's gate, Sam pausing long enough to close and lock it. From here the road angled northeast toward the fort. Their pace was determined by the team and wagon, with Harper pushing the horses as fast as he could.

Occasionally Bruce pulled to one side of the road or the other to ride to the top of a low ridge, and from there he used the glasses to scan the valley. Near noon he spotted a cloud of dust far to the south and west of Steens Mountain. He studied it for five minutes, noting that it was moving fast and coming in this direction, but he could not determine whether it was a band of Indians or a group of whites headed for the fort.

He returned to the party and reined in beside his father. He told him what he'd seen. Sam considered it a moment, then he said: "It's my guess it's Morgan and his crew coming to the fort. I don't believe the Indians will come any closer to the fort than they have to."

Half an hour later Jason, who had stayed behind much to Bruce's surprise, rode up to join Bruce and

Karen. "Better ride point for a while, Mister Bell," Bruce said. "You're eating a lot of dust back there."

"I'm the rear guard," Jason said, smiling slightly. "You know, I've learned a hell of a lot since we got chased into your hole in the ground. I'm surprised at myself 'cause I don't learn easy. I had it all worked out in my mind. Morgan Drew was the coming big man in this corner of the state and my daughter was going to marry him. Well, for one thing she's made it damned clear that she's going to marry the man she wants to and there's nothing I can do about it. Another thing I can't get over is Morgan lying to your pa. Only kids and cowards lie. A man don't have to."

"I'm glad you're . . . ," Bruce began.

Karen stopped him by reaching out and gripping his arm. She said: "Listen."

The three of them reined up. The wind was from the west and it took a moment for Bruce to hear what Karen had. It was rifle fire somewhere to the east. The only ranch out there was Verd Tucker's little ten-cow spread. The Tuckers were being attacked, and from the sound of the firing, the band of Indians was a big one.

"Tucker," Karen said. "Sue's there with him, isn't she?"

Bruce nodded, suddenly realizing that he had to make a decision and make it at once. Verd and Sue couldn't hold out very long against a big body of Paiutes. If he bought into the fight, the Indians might pull out, but he would leave his own party with one less gun to defend it if it was attacked. Everyone here except Donna had a rifle and could shoot. The Indians were not likely to attack a party of this size, as close to the fort as they were.

"Keep rolling," Bruce told Jason. "You ought to get to the fort in about two hours. Maybe less. I'm going to give the Tuckers a hand."

"I'm going with you," Karen cried. "I don't want to live if they kill you."

"No," Bruce said sharply. "I'll have a hard enough time staying alive without having to look after you."

She was hurt and she showed it, but he didn't apologize or look back after he rode away, not even when Jason Bell, outraged by this desertion, bellowed: "Stay here! That fight isn't your put-in. This is your outfit."

Bruce went on, putting Stony into a gallop straight across the flat through the sage. For a moment Jason Bell had held him in high regard, but he wouldn't now, Bruce thought ruefully. He had hurt Karen to boot. To make it worse, what he was doing would be a waste if he was too late to help Verd and Sue.

CHAPTER
TEN

Bruce drove Stony as hard as he could, knowing that time may already have run out on him. When he topped a low ridge east of the Tucker place, he looked down on the buildings and in a matter of seconds saw what had happened. The Indians had stolen Verd's horses and were driving them south, but a half dozen or more warriors were still firing at the house. Now and then a gun sounded from inside, a flash of powder flame streaking out of the window.

A shallow gully broke off the ridge a few feet to Bruce's right. He was too far away to do any good if he began shooting from here, and, although the gully did not offer much protection, it was the best he could see. He rode into it, left Stony behind a tall bank, and, pulling his Winchester from the boot, ran along the gully until it bent to the north away from the shack.

He eased over the bank and wormed his way through the sage until he was within fifty yards of the corral. The ground sloped away from where he lay, giving him a clear view of the shack. He spotted one Indian crouching behind a mowing machine, another flat on his belly under a wagon, and, although he could not see the others, he knew they were in the corral or shed.

84

As he studied the scene before him, Bruce became aware that no shots were coming from the shack. He opened up, knocking flat the Indian who was behind the mowing machine. His second bullet tagged the brave who was under the wagon, bringing him to his feet and half around. Apparently he was so surprised by this attack from the rear that he instinctively whirled to see where it came from. It was the last mistake he ever made. Bruce's third shot caught him squarely in the chest. He went down and lay there, not moving.

Bruce held his fire then, eyes searching for the others. The shooting stopped. A moment later four Indians broke out of the shed and raced away from Bruce past the shack toward a dry wash to the east. They were well on their way before Bruce saw them.

If Verd had spotted the fleeing Indians, he could have cut all four of them down, but he didn't fire. He was dead or out of ammunition, Bruce thought as he squeezed off a shot at the running Paiutes. They were hidden first by the shed and then by the shack, and, when they finally came into view, they were too far from Bruce for him to have much chance of hitting one. A moment later they dropped into the dry wash and disappeared.

Bruce hesitated a moment, thinking there might be other Indians in the shed, or if Verd didn't realize what had happened, he might shoot at anything he saw moving before he realized what or who it was. In any case, Bruce knew he couldn't stay here.

He sprinted to the corral, circled it, and reached the shed. The only door was on the side of the shack, but there were several wide cracks between the slabs. He took only a moment to find out that no one was inside. He eased around the corner in time to see the four Indians who had disappeared into the wash riding south in a dead run.

Bruce still hesitated to show himself, not knowing what shape Verd and Sue were in, so he stopped at the corner of the shed and yelled: "Verd! Sue! You all right?" When there was no answer, he called: "This is Bruce! Are you all right?" Still no answer. Both of them must be dead.

He crossed the yard to the shack on the dead run. The door had been riddled by bullets, the window beside it had lost most of its glass, and the entire wall had been peppered. Bruce pulled the door open and stepped inside. Verd sat on the floor, Sue's head in his lap. There was a bullet hole in the girl's head and Bruce saw at once that she was dead.

"They're gone," Bruce said.

Dried blood from a scalp wound made a dark streak down Verd's face. He looked up, but there was no expression in his eyes. Bruce squatted beside him and repeated: "They're gone."

"Gone." Verd repeated the word as if he wasn't sure what it meant.

"The Indians," Bruce said. "They're gone. It's safe to go outside."

Verd looked at his sister's face and gently patted her hair. He said: "She was just a year younger'n me. We took care of each other. Our folks died when I was fifteen. The neighbors was gonna put us in an orphanage or something, but we ran away. We made our own living after that. There was just the two of us till we came here and she met Morgan Drew."

"Verd, the Indians are gone," Bruce said. "Don't you understand? They got on their horses and rode away."

Verd stared blankly into space and went on as if he hadn't heard: "Just before they shot her, she told me she was going to have Drew's baby. She'd told him and he'd promised to marry her. That was two months ago, but he wouldn't see her no more and finally he wrote to her that he never wanted to see her again. After that she said she didn't care much whether she lived or died. I guess she knew she was gonna die or she wouldn't have told me."

"I'm sorry, Verd," Bruce said. "She was a fine woman."

"I quit shooting when she started to talk," Verd said. "I told her I'd make Drew marry her, but she said she didn't want to marry him under those conditions. She said if he didn't love her, she didn't want him. We were down on the floor and the bullets were flying above us. I'd jump up once in a while and shoot just to let 'em know I was still alive. But I didn't shoot no more after they got her. She started to say something about leaving the country 'cause she didn't want to see him no more and she couldn't stand folks talking about her and laughing at what had happened to her, and that was when she got it. She died right away. She didn't say anything else. She just fell over. When I got to her, she was gone."

For a long moment Bruce sat there, looking at Verd. The man was staring at the open door and Bruce was sure he didn't see anything. He was in a daze, so shocked by what had happened that Bruce wasn't sure he would ever come out of it.

"Verd, I'm going to get my horse," Bruce said. "When I come back, we'll bury Sue and then we'll go to the fort."

He didn't think Verd comprehended a word he'd said. He left the shack and strode back to where he had left Stony. Mounting, he rode to the shed and put the horse inside and stripped gear from him. He found a shovel in one corner of the shed and, picking it up, returned to the shack. Verd apparently hadn't moved.

"I'm going to dig her grave," Bruce said. "Where do you want it, Verd?"

He waited a minute or more, but Verd didn't look at him or say anything. Turning, Bruce walked out of the shack. He stood there in the hot sunlight not knowing what to do. Verd acted as if he were asleep with his eyes open. Bruce had never heard of anything like this before.

Suddenly he was aware of a long line of riders coming in from the south. He leaned the shovel against the wall of the shack and slowly walked toward them. The JB ramrod, Sundown McQueen, was the lead rider. As Bruce glanced back along the line of horsemen, he saw it was the JB crew.

McQueen reined up and signaled his men to stop. He looked questioningly at Bruce, then nodded at the two dead Indians. "What happened?"

Bruce told him, then added: "It's Verd I'm worried about. He doesn't seem to know what's going on. He ought to be taken to the fort so the doc can see him. Sue's got to be buried. We can't leave her body in the shack."

"I'll take a look at Tucker," McQueen said. "Having a thing like this happen is enough to make any man go loco."

They rode to the shack, Bruce walking beside McQueen's horse. He asked: "What happened to you and your crew?"

"We got caught," McQueen said grimly. "There must have been fifty, maybe sixty of the red bastards that tackled us, but we forted up in that old cabin of Red Smith's and fought 'em off. We was some worried about Jason and the women, but when we got to the house, there wasn't nobody there."

Bruce told him they were probably at the fort by now. They reached the door of the shack, McQueen motioning for the men to stop. He stepped down, saying to the man next to him: "Jingles, you 'n' me will take a look at Tucker. If anybody can bring him out of it, we're the ones who can do the job."

Jingles Nelson dismounted, glancing worriedly at Bruce. He said: "We don't want to bring him out of it too fast. Chances are he'll be trigger happy after what he's been through."

"I'll go in first," Bruce said.

When he stepped inside, Bruce saw that Verd apparently had not moved from the time he had left the shack. He said: "You've got company, Verd."

The blank expression remained on the man's face. It was unchanged after McQueen and Nelson came in. McQueen said: "We'll take care of Sue, Tucker. You go on to the fort and let the doc look you over."

Still Verd stared blankly into space. Bruce asked: "What made you think you two could bring him out of it?"

"We're the ones who worked him over the time he tried to settle at Skull Springs," McQueen said. "He promised to kill me the next time he saw me and I figured he'd try it. Looks to me like he's in bad shape."

"Maybe he can ride a horse," Bruce said. "You want to stay here and help me bury Sue?"

McQueen hesitated, glancing through the open door at the long stretch of sage flat to the south. He grimaced and nodded. "I don't want to, but I will. I just hope them red devils don't come back."

"Let's get him on a horse," Bruce said. "I don't know what we'll do with him if he can't stay in a saddle."

Bruce took one arm and McQueen the other, and they lifted Verd to his feet. He stood upright, not protesting and not looking at them. They led him outside, McQueen saying: "How about putting him on your horse? You can ride to the fort behind me."

Bruce nodded agreement and, after preparing Stony, brought him from the shed. "Verd," he said, "put your foot in the stirrup and climb aboard."

Verd obeyed like an obedient child, both hands gripping the horn, his blank gaze on the Blue Mountains to the north. He sat there, slumped forward like a rag doll. Bruce turned away, sick. He hoped that

Verd wouldn't start talking about Sue to the JB men. If he kept his mouth shut, no one else would ever know except Morgan Drew, and that, Bruce was sure, was the way he would want it.

"Lead his horse, Jingles," McQueen said. "We'll be in afore dark. If we aren't, you'd best come looking for us."

"We'll keep an eye out for you," Nelson said, and rode away, the rest of the JB crew following.

"Damned if that ain't a sorry sight," McQueen muttered, his gaze on Verd, who was swaying in the saddle. "I don't like him and he sure as hell don't like me, but that's got nothing to do with it. There's one more thing the Injuns have got to pay for."

Bruce picked up the shovel. "There's a fence around the garden, so we'd better bury her there. I'll start digging. You look around and see if you can find a tailgate of a wagon or something we can use for a head board."

He walked around the house, thinking it was Morgan Drew and not the Paiutes who would pay for what had happened to Verd Tucker, but that was something Sundown McQueen would probably never know.

CHAPTER
ELEVEN

Bruce and Sundown McQueen rode into Camp Harney late in the afternoon. The post was located on Rattlesnake Creek just below where it flowed out of its cañon in the Blue Mountains. Virgin pine grew on the slopes of the mountains to the north, and on the south the almost level floor of the valley was covered by sage and rabbitbrush, or by the water and tulles of shallow lakes and swamps.

The fort was divided by a wide, dusty road. On the left were the cavalry stables and the guardhouse, and a rifle range that lay some distance from the center of the post. On the right were the kitchens and mess halls, the slaughterhouse, the bakery, and the blacksmith shop. Beyond were the officers' quarters and the barracks enclosing the parade. Camp Harney was big. Also it was practically deserted.

Bruce and McQueen turned toward the store and saloon that had been built for civilians. Within a few minutes Bruce found his horse, and McQueen rode on to where the JB crew had made camp.

Bruce found his father's campfire. Mary was finishing supper as Bruce dismounted. She said in a shrewish tone: "Put your horse up. We're about ready to eat."

Bruce watered his horse at the creek and staked him out near the Holt wagon. The Daniels boys and their mother were camped not far away. Rick Rawlins and Cole Battles were eating with them.

Battles called: "I want to see you after supper!"

"That's good!" Bruce called back. "I want to see you boys, too."

When Bruce returned to his father's camp, Sam asked: "What happened at Tucker's place? I saw the JB outfit bring Tucker in. He didn't seem to be wounded, but he looked like hell."

Bruce told him what had happened, and added: "I've never seen a man act like that before."

"I did once," Sam said thoughtfully. "It was before we left the Willamette Valley. A neighbor got hit on the head. For days after that he walked around like he was asleep. He just didn't know what was going on. When you talked to him, he'd look at you like he didn't know what you were saying."

"What finally happened to him?" Bruce asked.

"He seemed to come to after while," Sam said, "but he couldn't remember anything that had happened between the time he woke up and time he'd been hit. I expect Tucker will come out of it after a while."

"I hope so," Bruce said. "Gives you a funny feeling, talking to a man who's looking right at you, and all the time you know he's not hearing a word you say. When I first went into the cabin, he talked a while, then he stopped and didn't say another word."

"What did he say?" Mary demanded.

Bruce hesitated, not wanting to tell her the truth. She would accuse him of lying about Morgan Drew, but more important was his certainty that Verd would not want anyone else to know about Sue's condition.

"Oh, about how they'd been fighting off the Indians," he said casually. "They were lying on the floor most of the time. He'd get up once in a while and shoot through the window to let 'em know he was still alive, then Sue got hit and he said she didn't say another word."

Mary turned away and wiped her eyes. She had not known Sue well, and Bruce doubted that she even suspected there had been an affair between Sue and Morgan Drew. She said: "Help yourself. The stew's ready."

"Ain't you gonna eat?" Sam asked.

"I'm not hungry," Mary answered.

"Why not?" Sam demanded. "You ain't had nothing since morning."

"I keep thinking about Sue," Mary said. "It could have been me or Karen. Or Donna Flagg."

"Yeah, it could've been," Sam agreed, "only it wasn't."

"You rode off and left us," Mary said accusingly to Bruce. "You talk so big about loving Karen, but you didn't stay and help protect her. Or Pa or me, either."

Bruce picked up a tin plate and filled it with stew. Karen and Jason Bell were probably sore at him, too, he thought. He didn't want to quarrel with Mary, so he said: "You're still alive." He hunkered by the fire and began to eat.

Sam filled his plate and poured a cup of coffee. He ate with great relish, and, when the sharp edge of his appetite had been satisfied, he said: "Some of the men don't have rifles, so when we first got here, we asked for some. There's only thirteen soldiers in the fort, you know. Most of the garrison is out chasing the Indians, and that's a damn' fool thing to be doing 'cause now they're behind the Indians. Nobody seems to know where they are or when they'll get back."

"Did you get the rifles?" Bruce asked as his father bent over the fire and refilled his plate.

Sam snorted in disgust as he squatted beside Bruce again. "Hell, they issued some carbines that wasn't worth a damn. Used them old linen cartridges, you know. Well, we took 'em out on the firing range and nobody could hit the side of a barn. We went back and told the soldier who gave 'em to us that they must have something better, and he admitted they did. This time we got some Springfields. We done purty good with them. But now ain't that a hell of a note, giving us them old no-good carbines in the first place? If the Paiutes had attacked us, we'd have played hob fightin' 'em off."

Bruce nodded, thinking it was the Army way. At least most of the settlers who had little use for the Army would say that. He put down his empty plate and refilled his coffee cup, then asked: "How many men are here? Settlers and buckaroos, I mean?"

"More'n fifty," Sam said. "There ain't enough Paiutes in the world to whip us if they tackle the fort, which same they won't. Morg, he's talking about all of us going together and trying to run the Indians down, but nobody else wants to leave our women here with only thirteen soldiers to protect 'em, so it looks to me like we'll wait till the companies that are chasing the Indians show up and then maybe some of the boys'll want to volunteer." He shook his head. "But not me. I'm going back to Rainbow as soon as I can. I'm like old Jason. I hope to hell they don't burn me out."

"Morg's here?"

Sam glanced at him warily. "Yeah, he's here. It was his outfit making the dust you seen this morning. The Paiutes jumped 'em and Morg dropped back and held 'em off." He looked down at his plate. "I know what you're thinking. You don't believe I've got enough guts to get him and old Jason together and see which one is lying. Well, I have. I'm going to do it first thing in the morning."

Bruce finished his coffee and flicked the grains that were in the bottom of the cup toward the fire. Sam had read his mind, all right. He still wasn't sure his father would actually do it.

"Where's Donna?" Bruce asked.

"Lieutenant Morton's wife took her in," Sam answered. "The lieutenant's gone and I guess his wife was kind of lonesome. Anyhow, they couldn't put her in the hospital. The doc says she'll be all right, but it was a good thing he got hold of her when he did or she'd have got blood poison."

Bruce rose. "I'm going to see Verd. He's in the hospital, isn't he?"

96

"Yeah, he's there," Sam said, "though what the doc can do for a man in his condition is something I don't know."

Bruce strode through the sage to the Danielses' fire, glancing back once to see Mary filling a plate with stew. Now that he was gone, she suddenly discovered she was hungry. She must hate him, he thought. She had no reason to, but it was typical of what Morgan Drew did to people. Probably the same thing had happened to Verd and Sue Tucker, a hatred that had been a virulent poison until the last few days, when Sue had finally realized Morgan wanted nothing more to do with her.

The Daniels boys, Rawlins, and Cole Battles had finished eating and were setting around the fire smoking when Bruce reached them. Rawlins said: "Bruce, we want to know what's wrong with Verd."

Bruce told them the same thing he had told his father and Mary, and all the time he kept wondering if Verd had talked at all after leaving his place. When he asked, Cole Battles shook his head. "He ain't said a word as far as I know. I asked Jingles Nelson and he said Verd didn't open his mouth all the way to the fort. After he got here, I was with him. He just sat there in the hospital, staring out of the window."

Rawlins nodded. "I was there, too. I've known Verd ever since him 'n' Sue came to the valley, but I never seen him like this before. I tell you, Bruce, it's enough to make a man get blind, staggering drunk."

"That's a good idea," Hank Daniels said. "I'll buy you a drink, Cole."

"No!" his mother said sharply. She turned from where she was washing dishes. "I'm afraid to be alone. Both of you boys stay right here with me. Don't you take a drink of nothing stronger'n coffee."

"Your ma's right," Rawlins said. "I'll stay here with you."

Cole Battles had been rolling a cigarette. Now he sealed it and put it into his mouth. Picking up a burning stick, he lighted it. He said: "Bruce, you 'n' me can go see how he is." He nodded at Hank Daniels. "I'll be back and roll my blankets up yonder on that soft place where the rocks are."

Hank chuckled. "I'll pound up a few of the rocks while you're visiting Verd so you'll have a soft bed."

Battles and Bruce walked through the sagebrush to the road and turned along it toward the hospital. Cole Battles was Bruce's age, a stocky man with a yellow mustache, pale blue eyes, and red hair. Like Rawlins, he was a bachelor who lived alone on the western side of the valley. As the years passed, he had become so furious at Morgan Drew's high-handed tactics that Bruce had expected him to resort to violence before this.

Now, as they walked through the twilight, Bruce sensed a change in the man. He wasn't ranting and raving and making all kinds of threats as he usually did. His mouth was hard set; the muscles at the hinges of his jaws were bulging as if he were holding marbles in his mouth. He was too subdued, and Bruce, glancing at him, sensed that he was holding a tight rein on his temper, but, when he lost control, he would blow up in an expression of murderous violence.

"What are you thinking, Cole?" Bruce asked.

Battles glanced at Bruce, giving him a tight-lipped grin. "I was thinking what a damn' fool I've been, talking like I was gonna egg Drew into a fight. He's here at the fort with about twenty men, and Jason Bell's got about the same. If there's a fight, old Jason will back him. There's been six of us. Now there's only five."

"You're thinking of Pete Daniels?"

"That's exactly who I'm thinking about. So's his mother and Hank and Rick. Pete ain't saying much, but once in a while you get a notion about what's going on inside him. With him, hating Morgan Drew ain't a thing to cuss about the way it's always been with me. It's something that's eating on him from way down in his belly. Sooner or later he's got to do something about it, but this ain't the time. That's why we're trying to keep an eye on him."

Bruce nodded. "It's that way with Verd. When he comes out of it, the first thing he's going to think about is killing Morg. Maybe it'd be better not to tell him the Big D bunch is here."

Battles threw his cigarette away. He stopped and put a hand on Bruce's arm. "McQueen and Nelson are the ones who beat Verd up that time. He's talked about shooting them and old Jason if he ever got a chance, but now you're saying he's going after Drew."

"That's right."

"Then something has happened we ain't heard about, something you ain't told us."

"I can't tell you," Bruce said. "It's up to Verd if he wants it told."

"Must be Sue," Battles said. "It's got to be. Turning Morgan Drew loose with women is like turning a stud horse loose with a band of mares."

They walked on, silent now. They reached the hospital and went in. "He's back here," Battles said, "unless they've moved him."

Bruce followed Battles into a small room at the end of the hall. In the thin light Bruce saw Verd sitting in a rawhide-bottom chair near the window.

"Don't look like he's moved since I was here," Battles said in a low voice.

Bruce crossed the room to him and laid a hand on his shoulder. He asked: "How do you feel, Verd?"

The man trembled, then his head turned slowly so he could see Bruce. His eyes were dull and expressionless as he asked: "Morgan Drew here?"

He spoke the three words in the thick-lipped way of a man who was drunk or asleep. Bruce said: "No, I haven't seen him."

"I'm going to kill him," Verd said, and, turning his head, stared out of the window.

He said these words in the same thick-lipped way he had spoken before. He wasn't trembling now. His shoulder felt as if his flesh had turned to stone. Bruce had a haunting feeling that this was Verd Tucker's body, but the real Verd Tucker was still back there on the floor of his shack with the head of his dead sister on his lap.

100

Bruce walked to the door and stood there waiting for Battles, who moved around to stand in front of Verd. "It's me," he said. "Cole. Remember?"

Verd didn't move or say anything or act as if he were aware Battles stood there. Battles shook his head and crossed the room to Bruce. They went into the hall and along it to the door, both men in a somber mood.

When they were outside, Battles said, his voice trembling: "Morgan Drew has a hell of a lot to answer for."

"He will," Bruce said. "The only question is when."

CHAPTER
TWELVE

Karen came to the Holt camp after breakfast Tuesday morning. She said to Bruce in her direct way: "I'd like to talk to you. Can we go somewhere?"

"Sure." Bruce glanced at Mary, who was washing the dishes, then at his father, who was hunkered on the other side of the fire, his eyes on the flames. "Pa, wait till I get back before you jump Morg."

"I'll wait," Sam said.

Mary looked up defiantly. "What do you think Morg's going to do, shoot all of us?"

"I just want to be sure he doesn't try," Bruce said, and took Karen's hand as they walked away.

"She's worried or she wouldn't think she had to defend him," Karen said in a low tone.

"So's Pa," Bruce said. "I guess they ain't quite as sure about him as they've been letting on."

As they passed the Danielses' camp, Hank elbowed Rick Rawlins and said: "Where do you suppose they're going?"

"Fishin'," Rawlins said.

"When I come back, I'm gonna knock your blocks off," Bruce said. "Both of 'em."

Hank and Pete Daniels guffawed, and Rawlins slapped his leg and howled. "Ain't love wonderful?" he said. "Ever see anything like it, Cole?"

Battles said: "Shut up, Rick. You, too, Hank." He rose and touched the brim of his hat to Karen. "You'll have to excuse 'em, Miss Bell. They didn't mean nothing. They just ain't too bright."

Karen didn't say anything or even look toward the Daniels camp. She walked beside Bruce, leaving her hand in his, her face turning so pale that the cluster of freckles on her nose and across her cheeks appeared very dark.

They were nearly to the creek before she said: "So that's your Ninety-Nine. I hope you do go back and knock their blocks off."

"Cole was right," Bruce said. "They didn't mean anything. They were hoorawing me and didn't think about insulting you."

"I never did like your friends," she said, "and I won't after we're married. I suppose they think you're consorting with the enemy."

"They probably would," he admitted, "but chances are they didn't think of that, either. Like Cole says, they ain't very bright."

She was still angry when they reached the creek. Bruce examined the ground for rattlesnakes, then Karen sat on the bank and took off her boots and stockings and dabbled her feet in the water.

The morning air was still cool, but the sky was clear, and the sun, rolling up above the eastern hills, would soon burn away the night chill.

Bruce filled his pipe and lighted it, watching Karen's elfin face, which was completely without guile. He couldn't guess why she wanted to see him, or whether she actually had a reason. He hoped she just wanted to be with him, but he was afraid there was more to it than that. She had always been direct and open with him from the moment she had come to him that afternoon on the JB and offered to ride Stony in the woman's race.

The silence ran on for several minutes. Karen leaned over the bank, frowning as she sloshed her feet in the shallow water that purred gently over the gravel bottom. The silence made Bruce uneasy because he knew he was expected to say or do something and he didn't know what it was.

Because he was puzzled, he said: "I love you, Karen."

She looked at him, her eyes filling with tears. "Oh, honey," she said softly, "that was what I wanted to hear. I'm such a goose. I had a horrible feeling you didn't."

"Why? Did I say . . . ?"

"No. I just didn't know what to think about your leaving us yesterday afternoon. I thought you didn't really care whether any of us reached the fort or not." She tried to laugh, but the sound was without humor. "Wasn't that crazy?"

Irritated, he said: "It sure was. What made you think a thing like that? Did Jason . . . ?"

"No. He yelled for you to stay there, but you didn't. I don't know why, but he admired you for doing what you did. After you'd gone a ways, he said I'd better marry you because you were a hell of a good man.

104

You've done something to charm him. I'm surprised because he never liked you and he was always pushing Morgan at me."

"He's finally seen through Morgan," Bruce said, "but I still don't savvy why you thought I didn't love you."

She turned her head to stare at the water. "I was scared. This is hard to explain, but we've all looked to you to give orders and work things out so we'd be safe. It's strange because I never knew father to do this with anyone else. You'd think we'd look to him, or Mister Holt, and even Long Tom. You were the youngest man in the whole bunch, but when you went galloping off through the sagebrush, I was terrified. I could see a whole big band of Indians jumping out of the next gully and killing all of us."

He shook his head at her. "Karen, I wouldn't have left if I'd had the slightest notion that would happen."

"I know that now," she said, "but when Mary saw you riding off, I think she was more scared than I was. She rode back to me and said there goes the man I thought was in love with me. She said you didn't think much of us or you'd stay with us until we got to the fort before you went sashaying off to get into a fight."

His hand gripped the bowl of his pipe so hard the knuckles were white. Mary did hate him, he thought somberly, hated him so much that she would do anything to hurt him, even to turning Karen against him.

"I guess we're all scared enough to be a little crazy," he said. "If I had waited until we got to the fort, Verd would have been killed. As it was, I got there too late to save Sue's life. I knew when I heard the shooting I didn't have much time, and the reason I took a chance and left you was because I figured the Indians wouldn't tackle a party as big as you were when we were so close to the fort." He took a long breath. Then he added: "Sometimes I feel like turning Mary across my knees and paddling her."

Karen took her feet out of the creek and ran her hands down her legs to rub off as much water as possible. She said: "We'd better get back to camp before your father gets tired waiting for us." She pulled on her stockings and boots and stood up. "I'm sorry and ashamed, Bruce. I know how it is with Mary. She realizes Morgan wants to marry me because I'm the only heir my father has, but I think she will do anything to get him."

Bruce got up and knocked his pipe out against his boot heel. He said: "I hope Morg pulls a gun on me. It's bound to come to that sooner or later, and it will save a lot of misery for all of us if it comes sooner."

Karen reached out and took his hand. "Bruce, I know you love Mary and it hurts you because she's turned against you, but have you thought that, if you kill Morgan, she will always hate you?"

"Yes, I've thought of that," he said, "but I've also thought that, if I kill him, he can't hurt Mary or Pa or anyone else. As long as he's alive, he'll hurt them along with a lot of other people. It's the way he is, Karen. He'll never change."

"He'll never change," she agreed, "but maybe killing him isn't the answer."

106

"Can you think of any other?"

"No," she admitted. "I can't."

When they reached the Holt wagon, Sam had let the fire go out, but he was still hunkered beside the ashes just as he had been when Bruce left. Mary was bringing a bucket of water from the creek. When Bruce glanced at her, she turned her face so she wouldn't have to look at him.

Sam rose, his face grave, his pulse pounding in his temples. He said: "Bruce, would you mind going after Morgan? And, Karen, would you fetch your father?"

Bruce glanced at Karen. When she nodded, he said: "Sure, Pa, we'll get them."

When Bruce reached the Big D camp, the cowboys were playing cards on a blanket or sprawled on the grass, smoking. Morgan Drew and Ben Louderman were not in sight. When Bruce asked about Morgan, one of the buckaroos said he was in the saloon.

Bruce found the two men sitting at a poker table, Morgan talking and pounding a fist into the palm of his other hand for emphasis. Louderman was grinning and nodding agreement. The instant Bruce pushed through the batwings, Morgan stopped, his head swiveling around to stare at Bruce, his expression hostile.

Ben Louderman was as different from Morgan as two men could be, and Bruce often wondered how they were able to get along as well as they did. Louderman had been a cowboy since he was ten years old. His legs were bowed, his face burned the color of old leather by wind and sun, and, although he was about Morgan's

107

age, he had a maze of wrinkles on his face, particularly around his eyes.

Louderman probably knew the cattle business better than anyone else in the country except Jason Bell, and he was good-natured about everything except animals. He was a small man, barely five feet six inches tall, but he was deadly when he saw someone abuse a horse or a dog.

"Howdy, Holt," Louderman said when he saw Bruce. "Come on in and sit."

"Thanks, Ben," Bruce said, "but I don't have time. Morg, Pa wants you to come to our camp for a minute."

Morgan shook his head, then changed his mind. "All right, I'll be over in a minute."

"Now," Bruce said.

Morgan scowled. He lifted his right hand to his forehead, and poked his clean, stiff-brimmed Stetson to the back of his head with his thumb. He said in an ominously low tone: "Ain't you taking purty long steps this morning?"

"Yeah, I guess I am," Bruce said. "I figured you'd want to shorten 'em up some."

"Aw, hell, Morg," Louderman said. "Go on. Our business can wait."

Morgan rose. "I guess it can."

Morgan shouldered through the batwings and strode across the sagebrush toward the Holt camp. Bruce caught up with him and walked beside him, neither speaking as they passed the Big D crew. Some of the buckaroos glanced at them curiously; others continued to play cards.

One thing was sure, Bruce told himself. There wasn't a man on the Big D payroll who wouldn't follow Morgan's orders whether it meant beating a boy like Pete Daniels almost to death or attacking Rainbow and killing everyone there.

This kind of loyalty baffled Bruce because it seemed completely irrational, but he knew it existed. The Big D buckaroos were not evil men. Still, they would do evil things if Morgan ordered them to. There simply was no middle ground when it came to people's relationship with Morgan Drew; you were for him or against him.

"You forgot what I told you about Karen," Morgan said out of the corner of his mouth.

"I sure did," Bruce said. "Why don't you make that order stick? Right now."

"You trying to prod me into a fight?" Morgan asked, still staring at the Holt wagon that was directly ahead of them.

"That's exactly what I'm doing," Bruce said. "When I was a kid and you knew you could whip me, you were always anxious to fight."

"I guess it's coming, all right," Morgan said, "and I ain't one to duck a fight with you. I can still whip you, but I'll pick the time and place."

They rounded the Holt wagon, Morgan touching his hat to Karen and Mary, who stood behind Sam and Jason Bell, a gesture that he managed to make gallant. "'Morning, Jason," Morgan said genially. "'Morning, Sam. Bruce tells me you want to see me."

109

He was suddenly transformed into the smiling, affable Morgan Drew, handsome, clothed in an aura of universal good will. Mary was starry-eyed, her gaze fixed on his face. Karen was grave, plainly worried about what was coming. Jason seemed to be amused, perhaps curious as to how Morgan would squirm out of this. Sam was self-conscious as if he were ashamed because he had bothered Morgan.

"I'm sorry about calling you from whatever you were doing," Sam said apologetically. "I suppose you were busy."

"Yes, I was busy," Morgan said with just the right amount of impatience, "but I'm here. What was it you wanted?"

"This won't take long," Sam said. "When you were at Rainbow Sunday morning, you told me Jason Bell was giving me one week, and then he'd make his move, but when the Indians chased him into Paradise Valley that night, he said you were lying."

Bruce expected Morgan to be embarrassed and get red in the face, to hedge and wiggle before he found a way to please everyone, but he didn't lose his aplomb for an instant. He laughed and slapped Sam on the back.

"Sure I lied, Sam," Morgan said heartily. "I didn't want to hurt your feelings. I like you and I ain't forgetting you were Dad's best friend. Besides, I owe you something for fetching me out to this country, but the truth is, I aim to have Rainbow. I'm going to get it one way or the other, but I won't cheat you, so I'm offering you a fair price."

110

He turned and strode away, a straight-backed, long-legged figure who moved with the easy grace of a huge cat. Jason watched him for a moment, then he said softly: "I'll be damned. He didn't want to hurt your feelings. Well, he's got gall and he thinks quick."

"I believe he meant that," Sam said gruffly. "About not wanting to hurt my feelings."

"He won't do anything, Pa," Mary said. "He was just trying to hurry you up about taking his offer."

"You're wrong about him not doing anything," Jason said. "Morgan isn't a bluffer." He pulled at his beard thoughtfully, then he said: "Holt, if he pushes you any more, let me know. I guess if our kids are gonna get married, it's time we started acting like neighbors."

"Thanks," Sam said, his brooding gaze still on Morgan's back.

Bruce didn't think his father fully comprehended what Jason Bell had said. He wasn't sure that he did, either. He had never really known Jason before, and the old man had not known him. Suddenly he had a feeling that even Karen had not understood her father.

Bruce held out his hand to Jason. "I want to say thanks for Pa and me. For Mary, too."

Jason shook hands, grinning a little. "It's all right, son. Don't thank me. I'm not above admitting I'm wrong once in a while. Not often, but once in a while."

He walked away. Bruce, looking at Karen, saw her lips tremble. She ran past him to catch up with her father. Watching them as they walked away toward the JB camp, Bruce told himself it was strange how you can live with a person all your life and still not know him.

When he turned to Mary, he saw that she hadn't moved. She still had the starry-eyed expression that just seeing Morgan always produced in her. As he walked away, the thought burned through his mind that Mary would still love Morgan Drew even if the man killed him and their father.

CHAPTER
THIRTEEN

The next three days were quiet, so quiet that Bruce told Karen a storm must be brewing. She said it had already brewed, that they were in the eye of the storm, and the first half had gone past.

"The second half will be here any time," she added, "and it'll be a lot worse than the first half."

He shook his head, thinking of Sue and Verd Tucker. "I don't see how it can be worse."

"Yes, it can," she insisted. "It can be a whole lot worse. You'll see."

He didn't know what she meant and he didn't press her. He was satisfied to accept these moments of peace and be thankful for them. He spent most of the time with Karen and realized more than ever how much he loved her, how much he wanted to marry her, but he knew they still had to wait. Karen knew it, too, and did not press him.

Sam stayed in camp, brooding and sour-tempered. Mary's disposition was even worse, for Morgan Drew carefully avoided both girls, claiming that he was very busy, although it seemed to Bruce that Morgan spent his time with Ben Louderman and their buckaroos, and could have seen either girl if he had wanted to.

Jason Bell drifted over to the Holt campfire several times each day to hunker by the fire and talk to Sam. On the surface at least he was a changed man, wanting Sam to feel he was sincere in his effort to be neighborly, now that he had accepted Bruce as a future son-in-law.

"Father is not a man to change his mind," Karen told Bruce worriedly. "This sounds ridiculous, but I wonder if he isn't afraid of Morgan. I mean, so afraid he's terrified."

"It's pretty ridiculous, all right," Bruce said. "He's got as many men as Morgan and plenty of money to hire more. Why would he be afraid?"

"I don't know," she admitted. "He tells me what a fine young man you are and he wants us to get married as soon as this Indian trouble is over. He's even offered to give me a wedding present of a thousand dollars so we won't have to wait."

"Well, now," Bruce said, grinning, "you'd better snap him up on that before he changes his mind."

She shook her head. "No, I don't want it. There's a string to it somewhere. I just haven't found it."

"Isn't there an old saying about not looking a gift horse in the mouth?"

"I know Jason Bell very well," she said. "I guess I know him better than anybody else knows him, and I can tell you that, as far as he's concerned, you had better look the gift horse in the mouth."

"I suppose he wants us to come to settle down on the JB," Bruce said, "and I'm supposed to ride for him and take McQueen's orders."

114

"No, he doesn't," Karen said quickly. "If that was the case, I might understand it, but he says he knows you'll want to stay with your dad on Rainbow. We can take the money and build onto the house or do anything we want to with it." She chewed on her lower lip a moment, then she added: "He said something else that doesn't make much sense. He told me you might want to use the money to hire more buckaroos for your dad, but you don't need any more, do you?"

"No," he said. "That does seem like a funny way to use a wedding present."

"That's what I thought," Karen said irritably. "I told you it didn't make any sense."

"Well, if he doesn't put some strings on it you can see," Bruce said, "we'll take the money and build a house of our own. That's the only way to start a marriage."

"We'd have to," Karen said. "I couldn't live in the same house with Mary. I've tried to make her like me, but I don't think she ever will."

"She doesn't like me, either," Bruce said. "I've told her too many things about Morgan. Talk about not making any sense. The way she acts is just plain loco."

"No, Bruce," Karen said, smiling. "I guess I wouldn't like anyone who said the things about you that we've said about Morgan."

In spite of himself he laughed, although what she said didn't seem relevant.

He went to the hospital every morning and afternoon to see Verd Tucker. Cole Battles went with him, and Rick Rawlins and the Daniels boys either accompanied

115

him or visited Verd some other time. Verd was always the same, acting as if he didn't know who his visitors were. He had a strange, far-away expression on his face, and, if he said anything at all, he'd say: "I'm going to kill Morgan Drew."

Bruce talked to the doctor about him Friday morning, but the doctor was completely baffled. "He eats and he sleeps," the medico said, "and the rest of the time he sits on that damned chair and just looks out of the window. He won't answer any questions. He's never said a word to me except to ask if Morgan Drew is in camp. I always tell him I don't know."

Bruce turned away, sick with worry, then swung back when the doctor said sharply: "Holt, we can't keep him here, you know."

"You'll keep him here till this Indian fracas is over," Bruce said harshly.

He walked away with Cole Battles, neither speaking until they were almost back to camp. Then Battles asked: "Well, who is going to take care of him if he don't come out of it?"

"I don't know," Bruce said. "I've sure been thinking about it. He can't stay by himself, and he doesn't have any relatives."

"We're the only friends he has," Battles said. "You 'n' me and the Daniels boys and Rick. Don't look like none of us can do it."

"Maybe Missus Daniels would if we paid her a little."

"No," Battles said, troubled. "She can't. Every time we get a little cold weather, she gets laid up with rheumatism. I've seen her flat on her back in bed, hurting so bad that she'd yell every time one of the boys tried to turn her over or help her sit up."

"I guess it's nothing we can decide now," Bruce said. "Cole, are you going to throw in with the Army and chase Indians? McQueen was telling me that Morgan's been talking it up with everybody but us."

Battles nodded. "I heard that, too. I don't figure it's my business to fight Indians if I can help it. That's what the Army's for. If you join the Army, you know that may be your job, but all I want to do is to get through that fence Drew and old man Bell put up and get me a better piece of land than I've got."

"It's the Army's job, all right," Bruce said. "Only thing is we know the country and I doubt their scouts do. Even Morgan doesn't know it as well as you do."

Battles nodded, his blue eyes narrowing and becoming hard and cold. "Now that I think a little more on it, I'll go along if you will. If I get a chance, I'll kill Drew. When there's a lot of smoke blowing around and yelling and shooting going on, who's to know whether it's my bullet or a Paiute's that beefs him?"

"Nobody, I guess," Bruce said, and walked on to his camp where Mary was getting dinner.

He was shocked by what Cole Battles had said, and yet he was convinced that Morgan Drew had to be removed just as a doctor would cut a malignant growth from a human body. Still, there must be a more honorable method than the one Cole Battles had suggested.

Sam Holt was hunkered by the fire, waiting for Mary to finish dinner. She did not speak or even look at Bruce as he came up and dropped to the ground beside his father.

"How's Verd?" Sam asked.

"No better," Bruce said.

Sam sighed. "Too bad. I thought he'd come out of it before now."

"You still figure on going back to Rainbow after the soldiers get here?" Bruce asked.

Sam nodded. "It's where I belong, not chasing Indians. If they're running the other way, I say we'd best let 'em keep on running."

"Only thing is they might swing around and head back here," Bruce said.

"It's a chance I've got to take," Sam said, "though I admit there's some danger in going to Rainbow now, mostly because we don't know for sure whether some of 'em might be hiding on Steens Mountain. If they are, they could hit Rainbow and take my hair and be gone before anybody knew it."

"I thought I'd go with the Army," Bruce said. "You don't care, do you?"

Sam gave him a searching look, then he said slowly: "No, I don't care, if that's what you want to do. The rest of your friends going?"

"Just Cole Battles."

"Bell was over a while ago and said him and Harper was going," Sam said. "He's sending the rest of his crew back to the JB. I guess with you and Battles, Morgan will have ten men."

118

"That'll help," Bruce said.

Sam cleared his throat and shot a glance at Mary. He lowered his voice to say: "Morgan asked Mary to go to the Big D with Louderman and the crew, and to stay there till the danger's over. He's sending most of the boys back, so she will be safer there than if she stays with me on Rainbow."

Bruce opened his mouth to say she'd be safer anywhere than on the Big D, but he didn't. He knew there wasn't any use. This was exactly what Mary had wanted for a long time, and Bruce doubted that Sam could keep her from going. She was eighteen, old enough to make her own decisions.

He stared at the fire, thinking grimly that finding an honorable way to remove Morgan Drew was not the point. The only thing that mattered was getting it done.

CHAPTER
FOURTEEN

Early in the afternoon someone raised the cry: "They're coming!" Immediately the settlers began streaming toward the parade ground.

Bruce and Karen were sitting on the creekbank. They rose and, looking to the south, saw the long line of cavalrymen coming in across the sage flat, a low cloud of dust marking their passage, the pack train bringing up the rear.

"I'll saddle up," Bruce said. "I don't think they'll be here long."

Karen caught his hands. "I want to kiss you good bye now," she said. "I'm not a woman who likes to have people watch her kiss the man she loves."

He grinned as he took her into his arms. "Don't worry about me. I doubt there will be any fighting. I'm like Pa. I think the Paiutes are better runners than fighters."

"Of course I'll worry," she said. "Even a running Paiute can shoot a man who's chasing him. I think you're crazy for going."

He shook his head. "It's Jason who's crazy. Why is he going?"

"I don't know," she said. "It has something to do with Morgan. Maybe he's afraid that Morgan will do more than he does or make him look bad or something."

He did not tell her what Cole Battles had said, but the thought had been in his mind that the same idea could work the other way. Morgan might want to kill Jason Bell, now that Jason had accepted Bruce as his future son-in-law. Jason was the only man in the country who had the power and the money to oppose Morgan effectively.

Bruce didn't want to worry Karen any more than she was already worried, so he said nothing about this. He would probably not be able to protect Jason if Morgan tried to murder him during the battle, but he would try, and he would talk to the old man about it when he had a chance.

He kissed her and she clung to him, crying a little, then she drew back, whispering: "I love you, Bruce. No matter what happens, remember that."

"It's the last thing I would ever forget," he said.

She whirled and ran toward her own camp, where her father was saddling his horse. Bruce's father and Mary were gone when he picked up his saddle and blanket and carried them to his sorrel. He had finished tightening the cinch and had swung aboard when Cole Battles joined him.

"Drew know we're tagging along?" Battles asked.

"I don't think so," Bruce answered. "At least I didn't tell him."

By the time Bruce and Battles reached the parade ground, the soldiers were riding in, a band of civilian scouts in the lead. According to the information Bruce had heard, General Howard would not arrive with the main body of troops for several days. This column was commanded by Captain Reuben Bernard, one of the most famous Indian fighters in the United States Army, having more than ninety fights with the hostiles to his credit.

The soldiers were dusty and tired and grim-visaged, but there would be no rest for them at the fort. Captain Bernard signaled the column to halt, and dismounted. Morgan Drew stepped forward and offered his hand.

"I'm Morgan Drew of the Big D," Morgan said. "Eight of us want to join your command until we're sure the savages are out of the country."

"Ten, Morg!" Bruce called. "Cole and me are going, too."

Morgan whipped around, glared at Bruce for an instant, his face turning red, then he wheeled back to face Bernard. "Ten, Captain," he said. "I didn't know these two men were going."

Bernard was a great bear of a man with a tremendous black beard. He shook hands, a trace of amusement in his eyes. "We'll be glad to have you and your men, Drew," he said. "You will take orders from Orlando Robbins, who is in command of my civilian scouts. Now where are the hostiles?"

Morgan stared blankly at him, then he blurted: "I don't know, sir."

"You have ten men who are volunteering to ride with us," Bernard snapped. "Why haven't you been finding out where the hostiles are?"

"We had a number of women and children here at the post," Morgan said. "When we got here, there were only thirteen soldiers to garrison the fort. We felt we should stay here in case the Indians made an attack."

"I see." Bernard's gaze swept the mass of settlers gathered along the edge of the parade, then brought his eyes back to Morgan. "We will be here only long enough to pick up rations. Be prepared to move out within the hour."

Bernard strode away as a leathery-faced scout approached Morgan. He said: "I'm Orlando Robbins. I'm glad to have you men in my command."

He shook hands with Morgan, then asked: "Who knows the country west of here?"

"Why, we all know it . . . ," Morgan began.

"I do," Cole Battles broke in. "I've hunted all through the Blue Mountains clean over on the head of the John Day past Crooked River."

"Then you're my man," Robbins said. "You'll ride beside me. Come here and let's take a look at this map. We camped near Crowley Creek along the north edge of Steens Mountain, then we moved onto the reservation the next night, but for all our weaving back and forth the last three, four days, we failed to pick up any fresh tracks. The captain figures they'll head west."

"That's what we all figured," Morgan said eagerly. "They'll probably . . ."

Ignoring him, Robbins turned to Battles. "I didn't catch your name."

"Cole Battles."

Robbins shook hands with him, then knelt on the ground and spread the map in front of him. Jason, standing behind Morgan, turned to Bruce and winked, his blue eyes twinkling. Bruce gave him a bare half-inch nod as Battles dropped to the ground beside Robbins.

"If they hole up somewhere in the cañons on Steens Mountain," Robbins was saying, "we'll have a hell of a time rooting them out, but if they head west and we can catch 'em before they get into the mountains, we'll give 'em a rough time. That's what we think they'll do. Some friendlies came into camp the night we were on Crowley Creek and said that was the plan."

For a time Battles's finger worked back and forth across the map as he explained the country to the head scout. Then he said: "I don't know how you plan to go from here, but the streams are high and some of the valley's under water. It strikes me we'd do better to swing north and keep on the high land. It's mighty swampy in the middle of the valley right now."

Both men rose. Robbins nodded thoughtfully as he folded the map and slipped it back into his pocket. He said: "I want to see the captain. We won't be here long. He ain't one to sit around when we're chasing hostiles."

As he strode away, Morgan Drew glared at Cole Battles, his hands fisted at his sides. If looks could have killed a man, he would have committed murder at that moment, but nothing was said. Presently Robbins returned.

"Battles, you 'n' me are riding out ahead of the column," Robbins told him. "If we don't pick up the trail by dark, I'm thinking they're still back yonder on the mountain somewhere."

Battles nodded agreement and stepped into the saddle. He lifted a hand to Bruce as he said: "Don't you wish you were important like me?"

"Well, no," Bruce said. "Go ahead and have your glory. The rest of us will do the fighting when the time comes, if you ever find the Indians."

"We'll find 'em," Robbins said, and rode west with Battles.

The column moved out half an hour later, Bernard giving the signal: "Forward, at a walk." Bruce caught Karen's face in the crowd and waved. He saw her wave back, trying to smile but not quite succeeding. He glimpsed Mary, too, but she was not looking at anyone except Morgan Drew. The last face Bruce saw was that of his father, grim and unsmiling as he lifted a hand in farewell.

A moment later they swung northwest, riding in a wide arc to follow the foothills. Bruce rode beside Jason, Morgan ahead of them with one of his men. He heard the varied sounds that a column of cavalry makes when it is on the move — hoofs striking against the hard, dry soil, the creaking of leather, the metal clacking of canteen and saber and spur chain, the murmur of horse-soldier talk running the length of the long line.

Bruce was glad he had decided to come. He would have a brief experience at soldiering. Like many settlers, he had little respect for the Army, and the few days he was with it would be enough. He told himself that it would be a good experience if it lasted only a few days. It was the kind of ordered life he could not endure for long.

"I was talking to one of the scouts while we were waiting," Jason said. "He told me Bernard had a hundred and sixty, Companies A, F, G, and L of the First Cavalry. Robbins has twenty scouts, so with us it makes a hundred and ninety men. That's a fair-sized bunch."

"You know how many Paiutes there are?" Bruce asked.

Jason shrugged. "There's a few of 'em, all right, but we can't even guess how many decided to go with Egan. I know for a fact that a lot of 'em didn't want to get involved in a war, including old Chief Winnemucca and his relatives."

"We'll find out in a day or so," Bruce said.

"I reckon we will." Jason stroked his beard, his gaze on Morgan's broad back, then he said out of the corner of his mouth: "That friend o' yours, Battles, he looks to me like a tough customer."

"He is," Bruce said. "I'm surprised that he hasn't opened things up before this." He hesitated, then decided there was enough noise to keep Morgan from hearing what he said. He leaned toward Jason, saying: "If we have a skirmish, watch your back."

"I aim to," Jason said. "You do the same." He was silent, his bright blue eyes turning ice-hard. "I never was a man to back off from anything or to change my

126

mind about my friends, but Morgan didn't give me a choice."

Bruce nodded, understanding what Jason meant. Only one thing really surprised him, the fact that Karen did not know her father as well as she thought. He had never given her a chance. Perhaps he would now.

That night they bivouacked at the base of the rimrock that formed the west wall of the valley. The stars came out and the cook fires were red eyes in the darkness. Bruce listened to the talk and laughter as he ate supper with Jason and Long Tom Harper.

Presently some of Robbins's scouts drifted up to smoke and talk. One of them said: "Funny thing about soldiers. They've been riding like hell and they know they'll have a fight in a day or two and some of 'em will get killed, but they feel good just to get away from the Army posts where they're bored to death."

Robbins and Battles rode in an hour later, Robbins reporting to Captain Bernard and Battles coming to Bruce's fire. He said: "We found their trail where they came out of the valley south of here. Two trails, really. One of 'em was made several days ago. That was the big party with a lot of women and kids. The other one was fresh. Robbins figures it was made by a war party. Maybe they'd raided some ranches for extra horses."

He paused, then added: "They've got a camp west of here, chances are. We won't have no trouble finding it. Judging from the tracks of the big bunch, there is one hell of a lot of 'em."

Later, with his head on his saddle, his eyes on the stars, Bruce thought that most of the Paiutes must have joined Egan's war party. For the first time he gave serious thought to what would happen to Karen if he and Jason were killed and Morgan Drew survived. He had to live, he told himself. He had to.

CHAPTER
FIFTEEN

The column was on the move again early in the morning, climbing out of Harney Valley to the sage-covered plateau and angling south until it picked up the tracks that the fast-moving war party had made. The scouts moved on out ahead of the cavalry, Robbins calling a halt only when he thought they might see the Paiute camp the next time they topped a ridge.

Robbins ordered his men to dismount and climbed a butte near the trail. He returned an hour later, saying he had spotted the camp in a grassy flatland not far away. He added grimly that it looked like a big band. At least there was a great number of lodges lined along the stream.

"That's Silver Creek," Battles told him. "If they're where I think they are, it's a purty good natural fort with lava walls on both sides of the cañon and some thick willows along the banks. I was hunting over there last fall and camped in that cañon. I can tell you we ain't gonna jump right down on top of 'em."

"I figured that from what I could see," Robbins said, "which means we've got to hit 'em from the ends of the cañon. We'll wait here till the captain comes up and see

129

what he says. No fires. There's too many of 'em to tackle unless we can surprise 'em."

They waited, some of the men sleeping, others gathering in groups to talk. Morgan Drew and his Big D hands sprawled on the ground near a clump of junipers, and Bruce, Cole Battles, Long Tom Harper, and Jason Bell remained together. It seemed to Bruce that the lines were clearly drawn, that once the Indian trouble was settled, Morgan and Ben Louderman would make their move.

Bruce thought about it for a time, and then said it plain out to Jason, and asked: "What are you going to do when they hit us?"

"Damn it," the old man snapped. "I've got a ranch to run. I can't run it if I've got to move my men to Rainbow and leave 'em to fight the Big D when they move in."

"I know that," Bruce said, "but, if there's just me and Pa on Rainbow, it wouldn't be much of a chore for Morgan to knock us off. What would you do then?"

Jason glowered at him, then he said: "I don't know. All I know is that Karen would hate me the rest of my life and I don't want that to happen. I've let her alone and taken her for granted too long." He stroked his beard, turning his gaze to Harper. "What do you say, Tom?"

"I say you can't afford to let Drew and Louderman have Rainbow," Harper said. "You need Rainbow just like it is now, same as you've got to have bacon between two slices of bread to make a sandwich. You'd best send

130

two, three men to help Sam until we know what's coming off."

"There's no sense to any of this," Jason complained in a cranky voice. "I don't know how it happened. A week ago I figured Morgan and me were good friends. Now I've got to scrounge around to keep the Big D from swallowing the JB."

"It ain't that bad yet," Harper said, "but it will be if Drew gets Rainbow. As long as he thought you was giving him your blessing as a son-in-law, he played it cozy, figuring that sooner or later you'd bring Karen around. Now it's plain even to him that Karen and Bruce are gonna get hitched and he can't stop 'em, so he'll be tougher'n a boot heel."

"Maybe I ought to talk to him," Jason said. "This country's big enough for all of us to live in without having to cut each other's throats."

"No," Bruce said. "I know how Morgan operates. You won't get anywhere talking to him. To your face he'll say you're right, the country is big enough for all of us, then he'll shoot you in the back if he gets a chance."

Harper nodded. "You should have seen this coming a long time ago, Jason."

"We had a deal," Jason said in an aggrieved tone. "I thought he'd keep his part of the bargain."

They were silent then, Cole Battles's gaze meeting Bruce's, and then turning away. Jason didn't say what the deal was, but there was no need for him to explain it. Bruce and Battles could guess. Jason and Morgan had built the fence to keep men like Verd Tucker off the good range land that the JB and the Big D were using.

As long as Morgan thought he could obtain the JB by marriage, he could wait, so he had kept his bargain. Now he had to use other methods. For all of Jason's wealth and power and toughness, he could not match the brutal ruthlessness that was a part of Morgan Drew. Bruce was certain that Jason knew it and that the knowledge weakened him.

Bruce filled his pipe and pulled on it while he held a match flame to the tobacco. As he watched the clouds of smoke disappear into the desert air, the thought occurred to him that they could just as well be living in another time and place when might was right.

This was the way it would be until the south end of Grant County was organized as a separate county. It could still remain the same, Bruce thought with a kind of desperate hopelessness. Morgan Drew by one devious device or another might be able to control the officials of the new county.

Jason rose and walked away through the sagebrush, his big shoulders slumped. Harper glanced at Bruce. "He's a hard man to tell anything to. Karen's talked to me enough so I knew what was bound to happen. I tried to tell Jason, but he was deafer'n a fence post."

Bruce, thinking it had been the same with his father and Mary, nodded. "I guess folks hear what they want to hear, no more and no less."

Cole Battles took off his battered Stetson and ran a hand through his red hair, his jaw set at a stubborn angle. He said: "I know one thing. If we get through this Indian scrap alive, I'm going to have my rights."

"Drew will make an outlaw out of you," Harper said.

"Then I'll be an outlaw," Battles shot back. "All I'm asking is that I get what the law says I can have. Anything wrong with that?"

Harper sighed. "Cole, there isn't nothing wrong with that according to theory, but it won't hold up in practice in the cattle country. Maybe it will twenty years from now, but not in Harney Valley or the Steens Mountain country in the year Eighteen Seventy-Eight."

"Then the law's a fraud," Battles snapped, "and to hell with it." He looked at Bruce. "You with me?"

"Don't listen to him, Bruce," Harper said sharply. "Once you start riding the owlhoot, you'll lose your home and Karen and everything else you want."

For a moment the image of Verd Tucker sitting on the floor of his cabin holding Sue's head in his lap was a stark, vivid picture in Bruce's mind. He said: "I'll go along with Cole if it comes to that, Tom. The law has got to mean something whether it's the year Eighteen Seventy-Eight or Seventeen Seventy-Six or Eighteen Sixty-One."

Harper sighed again, his long, lean face gloomy. He said: "Ain't this a hell of a note?"

Bernard's column did not arrive until after dark. He gave the order to dismount. Robbins talked to him a moment, then Bernard wrote a message that the war party of the hostiles had been located on Silver Creek, and sent a courier back to Camp Harney.

Bernard talked to Robbins for another minute or so, then both men strode to where Battles was waiting with Bruce and Harper. Jason had joined them again, a tired old man who probably wished, Bruce thought, that he had stayed at the fort.

"We'll attack in the morning," Bernard said. "Early. Before sunup. Robbins thinks this is the biggest gathering of Indians since the battle of the Little Big Horn, but, if we can surprise them, we won't wind up the way Custer did."

"We'll circle 'em and hit 'em from the upper end of the valley," Robbins added. "Battles, you'll guide Captain Bernard to the lower end. We'll start the ball. As soon as the captain hears our first shot, he'll move in with the soldiers."

"I don't like this," Jason objected. "We'll have less'n thirty men coming in from the upper end. If there's any delay on your part, we'll get wiped out before the cavalry gets there."

"You're running that chance," Bernard conceded, "but I've been through this a few times. I can promise you we'll be there. If it gets too hot, pull out. Don't let 'em box you in. You don't have to wait for my orders."

"The trick is going to be for us to keep moving," Robbins said. "That's why we've got to surprise 'em. They'll run for cover. I don't think there's any chance of them pinning us down."

"I've often wondered what the conversation was between Custer and his officers before the fight started," Bruce said.

"We'll never know," Bernard said, "but you know what *our* conversation has been. Battles, we'd better get moving, if you think you can get us into position in the dark."

"I'll get you there," Battles said.

Bernard and Battles wheeled and strode away as Robbins gave the command to saddle up. The scouts moved out a few minutes later, riding slowly and as silently as they could. Unless the Paiutes had warriors out covering a wide area, Bruce felt that the maneuver would be successful.

Apparently Robbins had mapped the country in his mind when he'd studied it from the top of the butte. Even in the darkness, his instinct for direction was faultless. Presently they angled toward Silver Creek, reaching it before the first hint of dawn showed in the eastern sky.

Robbins ordered them to halt and dismount, the word coming back along the line. Bruce had been riding beside Jason. They were near the end of the column, Morgan Drew somewhere ahead of them. For a moment Bruce was relieved by this position that had been a matter of sheer luck, but in the long run it meant nothing. The situation would change once the fight started. There would be no way to keep Morgan in front of them.

So they waited, the air cold and penetrating for June. Bruce shivered, and wondered if Bernard's men had reached their position. For a time Bruce heard no sound but the occasional stomping of a horse, the murmur of low talk, or the faraway call of a coyote from a distant rim.

Presently the day was born in the east, the stars died, and the light deepened enough to make out the junipers along the edges of the cañon and the mass of willows guarding the banks of the creek and the sheer walls on both sides of the scouts.

The order to mount came down the line. Bruce checked the cinch and stepped into the saddle. Leather creaked, a man behind Bruce swore for no reason except that it relieved the tension gripping him, and then the column began moving downstream toward the sleeping Indian camp.

CHAPTER
SIXTEEN

The Indian camp had begun to come to life. A few of the women had started breakfast, some of the men were looking after the horses, a number of children were playing along the creek, and here and there a dog sniffed around the cook fire looking for some tidbit that he had missed the night before.

A second later the entire situation changed into one of absolute confusion. Robbins yelled: "Gallop-ho! Let 'em have it!" He fired his revolver at a man who had just stepped out of the willows along the creek. The Indian dived back into the brush. The scouts thundered through the village, every man using his six-gun.

Some of the Indian braves fell and started crawling toward the willows. The women screamed and gathered the children and raced toward the nearest cover, brush along the bank of the stream or rocks under the rim. The Indians who had been asleep spilled out of their lodges, saw what was happening, and scattered in all directions like a flock of frightened birds.

Downstream from the village Bernard brought his cavalry into action in columns of fours the instant Robbins fired his first shot. Bruce heard the bugle and felt a great rush of relief. Cole Battles had succeeded in getting the cavalry into position and now the Indians were caught between two attacking forces.

For the first few minutes the Paiutes were so shocked by the surprise attack that they were confused, but in an amazingly short time they recovered and established a line of skirmishers. The best warriors were armed with new Winchesters. Now, having deserted the village, they hid in the brush and behind rocks and poured a withering fire at their assailants.

Robbins took his men through the entire length of the village. The cavalry swept past them and Robbins re-formed his men and charged back the way they had come. Bruce reloaded his revolver in time to fire pointblank at a half-naked warrior who leaped out of the brush to grapple hand to hand with Cole Battles. The Paiute threw up his hands and sprawled full length on the ground, got to his hands and knees, and started to crawl back into the willows, then suddenly collapsed into the grass.

Bruce had a feeling that order had turned into anarchy. The gunfire was deafening; the echoes thrown back by the cliffs on both sides of the creek were almost as bad. Bullets snapped all around Bruce, one slicing through the crown of his hat.

Smoke rolling across the valley was so heavy that it became impossible to see what was going on. Through all the thunder of firing sounded the yells of men, some in agony, some in frenzied oaths, and other cries that seemed to be the meaningless expression of fighting men caught in a melee that aroused their instinctive fury but was beyond their comprehension.

Several of the Indians who were on horses raced across the valley. Bruce recognized Egan, the Paiute war chief, who dropped to the far side of his pony and fired at Robbins. The scout, shooting back, knocked Egan off his horse.

Robbins's horse was hit, and Bruce, coming up fast, fired at Egan and hit him, but he saw at once that the chief wasn't dead. Before he could pull the trigger of his revolver again, a great wave of warriors erupted from the brush and Bruce was forced to veer away. The Indians carried Egan into the safety of the thick-growing willows before he could be hit again.

Now the hostiles had rallied enough to pour a fire at the whites that was so fierce it was suicide to remain in the open. Bruce heard the bugle sound "Cease Fire" and "Recall." Both the cavalry and the scouts fell back to where Bernard thought they could safely fort up.

The men pulled saddles off their horses and tied them, forming a picket line. Quickly they rolled rocks into a crude semicircle that furnished some protection.

Bruce, finding himself beside Robbins, said: "Looks to me like we're pinned down whether Bernard thought it could happen or not."

"We can get out of the valley if we have to," Robbins answered, "but I don't think the captain wants to."

"Suppose the Indians circle us and close the end of the cañon?" Bruce asked. "We may be here to stay."

Robbins shook his head as he studied the Indian position on the far side of the creek. There was very little firing now. Some of the soldiers and scouts had taken money and ammunition and odds and ends that attracted them from the deserted camp. All the Paiutes could do was to yell at them and waste a few bullets.

"It's my guess the redskins want to do just one thing," Robbins said. "That's to get out of here. They were running when we caught 'em, and they'll keep running."

"Seems funny we surprised 'em," Bruce said. "They must have known the soldiers were after 'em."

"They didn't think we were as close as we were," Robbins said. "There are a lot of funny things about Indians. Sometimes you think they're real smart and other times they're like children and don't look ahead no farther'n the end of their nose. I've known a lot of times before this when you'd think they'd put out guards to warn 'em if they was attacked, and didn't do it."

The silence seemed strange after the thunder of battle. Apparently the Indians were satisfied to carry off their dead and bandage their wounded. The soldiers and scouts took advantage of the lull to roll more rocks in front of them and dig shallow trenches back of the stone breastworks.

Cole Battles dropped down beside Bruce and winked at him. "Well, you've had a taste of Indian fighting. How'd you like it?"

"I thought it got a little hot there for a while," Bruce said. "I'm glad Bernard doesn't think he's Custer. We could have taken a good whacking if we'd stayed out there where we were."

"He's a good man," Battles agreed.

"I don't know what we accomplished by making this attack," Bruce said thoughtfully. "We lost some men and quite a few horses. Bernard doesn't have a big enough outfit to keep on their tail, so it looks to me like they'll pull out and Bernard will have it to do all over again."

"We hurt 'em purty bad," Battles said. "They've lost their camp and a lot of stuff went with it. If they get away, they ain't likely to pick up as much as they lost this morning."

"They've got us outnumbered," Bruce said. "If they decide to attack, it'd be hell on high red wheels."

"Yeah, but I don't think they will," Battles said. "All I know is that Bernard aims to sit tight till Howard gets here with reinforcements. Bernard thinks there was about two thousand people altogether in camp. You can figure one third of 'em was warriors, so he ain't gonna push too hard till he has more men. Besides, the soldiers were running short of ammunition. I think that's the main reason we pulled back."

"If the Paiutes take out and run from here," Bruce said, "it's a pretty sure guess we won't see 'em in the valley again."

"That's right," Battles agreed. "If they're gone in the morning, we can head for home."

The hours passed slowly, with only sporadic shooting. The sun rose to high noon and tipped on over toward the west. Once Robbins stopped to talk, saying: "It's gonna be a long ride before we stop 'em for good. Howard may not get here for a couple of days. We got one prisoner, an old woman who says they're going on through the Blue Mountains to the Umatilla Reservation, which is what we guessed all the time. They expect to pick up some discontented Cayuses and Umatillas, and they probably will if we don't stop 'em first."

"There'll be some dead settlers," Battles said.

Robbins nodded. "The captain knows that. It's the worst part of the whole business, but we don't have the supplies or ammunition to keep on their tail even if we had enough men."

Later in the afternoon Long Tom Harper squatted on the ground beside Bruce and Battles, his gaunt face gloomier than ever. He asked: "You seen Jason?"

"Not lately," Bruce said. "I thought he was with you." He considered a moment, then added: "Come to think of it, I haven't seen him since the fight started. I was beside him when we made the first charge. After that we got mixed up. There was so much smoke and switching around and everything, I guess I didn't even think about Jason."

"I didn't see him go down," Battles said. "If we had any wounded or dead men in sight, we fetched 'em in."

Harper waved a hand upstream. "There's a lot of brush along the creek. It'd sure be easy to hide a man's body."

Bruce looked at Harper, then at Battles, certain that the same thought was in all their minds. Now that it was too late, he wondered why they hadn't watched the old man during the fight. He knew at once it was a foolish question. It would have been impossible to

142

watch Jason during the few minutes of wild excitement when the battle was at its hottest.

"You seen Drew lately?" Harper asked.

Bruce and Battles shook their heads. Bruce said: "I don't think there's any Indians along the creek now. We'd better start looking before it gets dark. Tom, go tell Bernard what we're going to do so we won't get shot."

Harper nodded, and ran along the rock wall to where Robbins and Bernard were talking to Private George Foster of Company L, who had been wounded severely. He returned a moment later, saying Bernard told him to be back before dark because anyone moving out there in front of the breastworks would likely be fired at if the troopers couldn't see who it was.

The three men slipped over the rock wall and raced toward the screen of willows, taking a zigzag course in case the Indians saw them and started shooting, but it was an unnecessary precaution. They reached the creek without a shot being fired and dropped flat to recover their breath.

Again the sense of guilt lay like a heavy burden on Bruce. This was a tragedy they had foreseen. Somehow, even in the commotion and the wild insanity of battle, they should have been able to prevent it.

They began moving upstream, Bruce not doubting for a moment that they would find Jason Bell's body along the bank of the creek hidden in a thick growth of willows.

CHAPTER
SEVENTEEN

They found Jason in less than an hour. He had crawled through the brush and laid next to the bank, motionless, his eyes closed. Bruce, who was the first to see him, called to the others and knelt beside Jason, thinking he was dead. Blood had dribbled from the old man's mouth onto his white beard and had dried there, making an ugly brown stain.

Jason stirred and opened his eyes. "'Bout time you got here," he whispered. "I ain't gonna last much longer. They shot me in the back. I've been wondering whether you'd get here before I cashed in."

Battles and Harper were there then, Harper asking: "Was it Drew that plugged you?"

"I dunno," Jason said. "I don't want to go to hell accusing the wrong man. I was chasing a Paiute. I hit him, but he kept going. It was during the worst of the fighting. I didn't hear the shot that got me. I didn't see who fired it, neither. It felt like a club hit me in the back. I was out cold for a while. I dunno how long it was. When I came out of it, I looked up and there was Morgan sitting his saddle and watching me."

Harper swore. "He knowed you was shot and he didn't fetch you in?"

144

"I told him I was hit bad," Jason said. "I asked him to get me back to our lines if we had any. I could still hear some firing. He didn't say a word. He grinned a little and turned his horse and took off out of there."

"We'll get him, Jason," Harper said in a low tone. "We'll get him and we'll hang him."

"No," Jason said. "I've had a lot of time to lie here and think about all I've done and mostly of what I didn't do. Like they say, a drowning man sees his life in a few seconds before he cashes in. I know one thing. You can't hang him for me 'cause I don't know he shot me. He'll keep going 'cause he can't stop. He's bound to make a mistake. You wait and get him when he does."

He closed his eyes and was silent for a time. Bruce thought he had stopped breathing. "We've got to get him out of here," Bruce said. "Maybe he's not hit as hard as he thinks."

"His horse is upstream a piece," Battles said. "I'll fetch him."

"Wait," Jason said. "I know how hard I'm hit. I ain't a praying man, but I done some praying today. I wanted to live till you got here, Bruce. I've got to tell you something. I see everything different now than I did before, and I'm ashamed of myself. About the way I treated Karen's ma and the way I've treated Karen. Marry her, son. Marry her right away. She'll find my will in the safe in my office. I ain't leaving her much money, but the JB is all clear and you won't have no trouble making a living."

Battles slipped back through the willows to get the horse. Bruce said: "I aim to marry her, Jason. I love her."

"I know you do," Jason said. "I know she loves you. But don't wait. I never saw through Morgan till I got to your place and your pa told me how Morgan lied. Seems like my eyes was opened then. It jolted me and made a different man out of me, I guess. I want you to marry Karen because she can't stand up to Morgan alone. I figure you can, Bruce. Maybe you're the only one who can."

Jason took a labored breath that shook his great body. He went on: "I stayed alive to say this, Bruce. You tell Karen I love her and I'm ashamed I wasn't a better father to her. Maybe a man don't know what's important till he's fixing to die. I never bothered to neighbor with your pa. I didn't think he was worth it. There was just me and Morgan Drew, but it was root hog or die with him all time. He never was honest with me."

That was all Jason had to say. He lay motionlessly, his eyes closed. Bruce felt for his pulse, then looked at Harper. "He's barely alive. Think we can move him?"

Harper nodded. "Nobody can do anything for him here."

They carried him through the willows and waited until Battles led Jason's horse to them. He said: "This animal was a mite skittish and I had a little trouble getting hold of him." He looked at Jason, then at Bruce. "Is he dead?"

Bruce felt of his pulse again, but this time he could not feel the slightest throb. "He's gone." He stood up and wiped a hand across his face. "I've heard of people who wouldn't die for one reason or another, but I never believed it."

"You can believe it now," Harper said. "With that hole in his back, I don't know how he lasted this long." His hands fisted at his sides, the corners of his mouth twitched as he stood staring at the dead man. "Let's go get Drew."

"No," Bruce said. "Jason was right. We don't have any proof he fired the bullet that got Jason."

"We don't need any proof," Harper said. "It's enough that he was here and saw Jason and didn't do nothing for him."

Bruce glanced at Battles, uncertain for the moment. Battles said: "I know what you're thinking. There's six of them and three of us. No good gambler bucks odds like that. We'll wait till we get better odds."

"Let's take him in," Harper said, unconvinced. "It'll be dark if we don't."

They lifted the body to the saddle, lashed it down, and with Harper leading the horse, they returned to the rock wall. A number of men gathered around them as Harper untied the body. He eased it to the ground, then covered it with a blanket. Bruce, standing beside Harper, scanned the civilians and saw that Morgan Drew and his men were not among them.

When Robbins came up, Harper asked: "Where's Drew?"

"He pulled out while ago," Robbins said. "Told us there wouldn't be no more fighting and we wouldn't need him and his men."

So he was gone, afraid to face Jason's friends when they found out what had happened to him. Or perhaps he had not wanted a showdown here. He told Bruce once that he would pick the time and place for the fight that both knew was inevitable. Morgan had no way of knowing what Robbins and his men would do if they learned the truth, or even Bernard and his troopers, so the safest thing had been to pull out.

"We'll wait till morning," Bruce said. "If they don't attack, I don't figure you'll need us, either."

"I reckon not," Robbins agreed. "I look for 'em to start moving tonight. Anyhow, we'll know, come morning."

The twilight faded into darkness, cook fires made an irregular semicircle inside the breastworks, supper was cooked and eaten, and all through the activity a pall of silence lay upon the camp. Brave men had died and others were wounded, and no one knew what the Indians would do in the morning.

The Paiutes might try to storm the breastworks before sunup in the hope of recapturing their camp and the supplies they had lost. They might even circle to the top of the lava wall and from that position they could pour a devastating fire upon the camp that would make the soldiers' position untenable.

Bruce slept fitfully, although weariness was like a drug that slowed his body processes until he found his thoughts coming slowly and sometimes even irrationally.

148

There was a dream, too, that somehow got mixed up with his thoughts.

He saw himself walking toward Morgan Drew, then he saw Morgan coming toward him, and he knew that one of them would kill the other. He heard Mary's frantic scream: "No, Bruce! Don't kill Morgan!" He woke up, shivering, not knowing who killed who, then he dropped off to sleep, only the dream came again. Both times his sister never told Morgan not to kill Bruce.

The camp woke with the sun. The Indians had kept a big fire burning all night, but they were gone long before daylight came to the valley. Robbins said: "I figured they'd do that. They must have gathered a lot of sagebrush and left a few bucks behind to keep the fire going so we'd think they were still there. Chances are they skinned out the minute it was dark."

As soon as they finished breakfast, Bruce, Battles, and Harper saddled their horses and tied Jason's body across his saddle. They shook hands with Robbins and Bernard, Battles offering to stay if they still needed a guide.

"It won't be necessary," Bernard said. "We've been studying a map. The hostiles will almost certainly take the shortest route to the south fork of the John Day and follow it north. It'll be slow going for them with their stock and women and children. We'll move to the site of old Camp Currey and wait there for General Howard, then we'll start after them again."

"You won't have no more trouble in Harney Valley," Robbins said. "Thanks for your help."

"It was our fight, too," Bruce said.

They rode out of camp, Harper leading Jason's horse. They followed the creek until they were clear of the cañon, then Harper said: "You reckon we'd better head for the fort?"

"I've been wondering about that," Bruce said. "Karen is probably still there, though your guess is as good as mine."

"It ain't much out of the way," Battles said, "seeing as a lot of the valley is under water. I say go to the fort. I want to see Verd." He shot a glance at Bruce. "You never did tell what made him go out of his head the way he done."

"He's the one who'll have to tell you if you're ever told," Bruce said. "I want to see him, too. I've got a notion Pa's gone back to Rainbow. If Karen's left, we'll have to take the body on south tomorrow. Chances are we will anyhow because she'll want Jason buried on the JB."

"Sure she will," Harper said. "All right, we go to the fort, but tell me one thing. How do we get at Drew? He'll be home with twenty men to fight for him if it comes to that."

"It'll come to that," Bruce said. "The question is when and where. Chances are that, if we go sailing into the Big D after him, we'll get shot to hell. I don't see much advantage in that. We'll talk about it after the funeral."

"Then I suppose you'll say we wait," Harper snapped. "Oh, no, we ain't waiting. We'll have the

150

funeral, all right, then, if I'm any judge of Sundown McQueen, we'll go after Drew."

Bruce didn't say anything because he knew it was no use to argue. Later, maybe, but not now. They rode in silence, taking the most direct course toward Camp Harney they could. There must be a legal way to get at Morgan Drew, and the first thing that had to be done was to take down the fence, but Bruce wasn't sure if Harper and McQueen and the rest of the JB crew would stand still for that, or even if they would take Karen's orders.

What would Cole Battles and Rick Rawlins and the Daniels boys do? And Verd, if he had recovered? Bruce stared at the rolling, sage-covered desert ahead of him, knowing that nothing was settled, that Jason Bell's death had only added to the uncertainty.

CHAPTER
EIGHTEEN

The first thing Bruce noticed when he came in sight of the fort was that the camp site was deserted. The settlers were gone. He swore and turned to Battles. "I suppose they thought that the Indians were whipped the minute we moved out with the soldiers."

Battles nodded somberly, his gaze sweeping the creek where there had been a long row of horses and rigs and a few tents. Not one was left.

"Even the fool Daniels boys took their mother back home," Battles said. "It was all right if Rawlins wanted to risk his hide, but Missus Daniels should have been left here. There's no way under the sun for them to know for sure that there ain't a few renegade Paiutes holed up somewhere on Steens Mountain."

"I ain't surprised at Karen going back with the crew," Harper said. "There's enough of 'em to protect her, and I reckon Mary's on the Big D with Ben Louderman."

"That's a good guess," Bruce said in a tight voice. "I don't suppose Pa could have stopped her if he'd wanted to."

Harper gave him a sharp glance. "Maybe we'll go sailing into the Big D, after all, and get shot to hell."

"Mary's of age," Bruce said. "I've done my damnedest to tell her what Morgan is, but she's old enough to do what she wants to do."

"We'd better get her out of there," Harper said.

"No. I told you she's of age." Bruce paused long enough to get his temper under tight control. Harper wanted a fight because of what had happened to Jason. He'd get it, but Bruce wasn't going to have it triggered over Mary. "There comes a time when every man or woman has to live by their own decisions. Mary's got so mad at me on account of what I've said about Morgan that she wouldn't speak or get me anything to eat. If she's on the Big D, you couldn't drag her out of there."

"If she was my sister . . . ," Harper began.

"Shut up!" Battles said hotly. "In the first place, she ain't your sister. In the second place, you don't know nothing about it. I think I do because I've heard Sue Tucker quarrel with Verd about Drew. I don't know what there is about that bastard, but women don't reason when they think of him. They just want to be with him. The ones who think they love him, I mean. I reckon Sue did and Mary does."

Harper held his tongue then, his mouth a bitter line across his gaunt, dark face. When they reached the creek where they had camped, they dismounted, Harper easing Jason's body to the ground and covering it with a blanket.

"I'll go buy some grub," Harper said, glancing at the sun, which was almost down. "I'd like to take the body to the JB tonight, but the horses are tuckered out and so am I."

153

"I'm going to see Verd," Bruce said. "I'll be back in a little while. I want to find out if he's got his sense back yet."

Battles hesitated, then he said: "Go ahead, Bruce. I'll take care of the horses. If he's all right, fetch him over here with you. We'll rustle a horse and saddle for him someway."

Bruce crossed the creek and strode toward the hospital, half running before he got there. The doctor must have seen him coming because he stepped outside and called: "If you're looking for Tucker, you can slow down! He's gone."

Bruce stopped ten feet from the medico, staring at him blankly. "Did he come out of it?" Then he caught the tight-lipped expression on the doctor's face, and asked: "What happened?"

"I don't know what happened," the doctor said irritably. "He ran off. That's all I know. You put yourself out for a damn' settler when you know he's too poor to pay you and you've got no business taking him in anyhow, then he just ups and disappears without saying thank you or go to hell or anything."

"I don't savvy," Bruce said. "If he wasn't all right, why did he leave? I mean, I didn't think he would."

"I didn't, either," the doctor said. "Of course I'm being unfair. The man's out of his mind. We didn't put a guard on him. I just never dreamed he'd do anything like that even if he could. He acted the same as usual the rest of the afternoon when you left with Captain Bernard, except that he ate a good supper. Sometime after dark he sneaked out of the hospital, crossed the creek, and stole a horse, a saddle, a rifle, and a revolver."

"He couldn't," Bruce said. "Why, there were forty men or more strung out along the creek. Somebody would have seen him."

"I tell you it's what he did," the doctor said doggedly. "He must be part Indian. I've heard of them doing stunts like that. Anyhow, he crawled into the camp of the Big D men and he stole Ben Louderman's revolver right out of his holster. He picked up another man's rifle and got out of their camp, then he saddled a horse that belonged to a settler from up north, and took off. Nobody knew what happened until morning."

If the circumstances had been different, Bruce would have laughed. Probably Ben Louderman had been sleeping off a load of whiskey, but still it had been a good trick and one that would have tickled Verd if he had been his normal self. Then the thought struck Bruce that maybe he was, that he had been pretending all this time.

No, not all the time. Not at first, anyhow, but he might have come out of it hours or even a day after he had been brought here and decided he'd keep on playing the game, that it was a sort of disguise that would give him a freedom he would not have in his normal state.

"I don't suppose anybody knows in which direction he went?" Bruce said.

"How could they?" the doctor asked petulantly. "He just disappeared, but I'll tell you one thing. If they ever catch him, they'll hang him for horse stealing.

Louderman will hang him for taking his revolver. You never saw a madder man than he was the next morning."

In spite of himself, Bruce grinned. Nothing would make a man lose face more than the theft of his revolver while the gun was in his holster. Bruce had always thought of Ben Louderman as a banty rooster, a man who could not bear the loss of his dignity.

"I'll thank you for Verd," Bruce said. "He's not an ungrateful man ordinarily." He turned away, then swung back. "How's Donna Flagg?"

"She's doing fine," the doctor said. "She'll be here for a while yet, but it's just a matter of the wound healing."

When Bruce returned to camp, he found that Battles had a fire going and Harper had started supper. Bruce filled his pipe and hunkered by the fire as he told them what he had learned. Even Harper, as taciturn as he was, could not restrain the grin that tugged at the corners of his mouth.

Battles laughed so hard he was out of breath. "I wish I could have seen old Ben when he woke up and missed his shooting iron. I'll bet he was swinging his arms and jumping up and down and thinking of new cuss words."

"You can likewise bet he took some rawhiding from his buckaroos," Bruce said. "He'll be a long time living that down."

Harper scratched the back of his neck. "You boys know Tucker better'n I do. Where do you figure he went?"

Bruce and Battles exchanged glances, neither wanting to say what was in his mind. Bruce was as certain as he could be of anything as vague as this that Verd had struck off for Steens Mountain and he would hunt Morgan Drew the same as a man would hunt a sheep-killing dog.

"Chances are he went home," Bruce said. "He probably couldn't stand that hospital room any longer."

"We'll stop at his place tomorrow," Battles said. "We'll find out what shape he's in."

There was no trace of Verd Tucker when the three men stopped at his cabin the next morning. Bruce was sure he had been there because the shelves behind the stove had been stripped of food. He went outside to where Battles and Harper were waiting, Harper impatient to get under way again.

Bruce stepped into the saddle and they rode south, no one feeling like talking. If Bruce knew the shape Verd was in, he would have felt better, but he realized that even a madman sometimes has a talent for doing sly and devious acts. The fact that Verd had stolen Ben Louderman's revolver from his holster did not prove he was his old self.

They reached the fence and Bruce stepped down, opened the gate, and shut it again after the other two rode through. He was tempted to talk to Harper about the fence, but told himself it was not the right time, that Harper had only one thing on his mind, to deliver Jason Bell's body, have the funeral, and start after Morgan Drew.

When they reached the place where Bruce and Battles turned off to go to Rainbow, the three men reined up. Bruce said: "Let me know when the funeral is, Tom. I want to be there."

"It won't take long to bury him," Harper said impatiently. "You gonna be at Rainbow?"

"It depends on Pa," Bruce said, "but I expect to be there."

"I'll let you know," Harper said, and went on.

Bruce turned toward Rainbow, Battles riding beside him. Once Bruce glanced at Harper, who was riding at a faster clip now, leading Jason's horse and hurrying him along as if he had run out of time.

Strange, Bruce thought, that he had lived beside Jason Bell for eight years and yet it had been only in the last few days that he had learned to know the man and to like him. He wanted to see Karen, to comfort her and tell her what Jason had said before he died, but it would have to wait until the funeral. Now the job was to find Verd Tucker.

"I'd like to see if my shack's still there or if them red devils burned it," Battles said, "but I guess I'd better go along with you."

"Verd may be dead by now," Bruce said. "I wish we'd stayed at the fort and looked after him."

"How could we?" Battles asked. "Unless we'd stayed right there in the hospital, we couldn't have done anything. We wouldn't have done him any good because we wouldn't have known about it till morning."

"I guess not." Bruce paused, then he added thoughtfully: "I suppose we could have told Harper

158

where we thought Verd went, but he'd have used it as an excuse to hit the Big D."

Battles laughed shortly. "Kind o' funny. Harper is sort o' slow and easy-going and all, but here he is, wanting to jump in and get himself shot. Me, well, I guess folks have always called me reckless and spoiling for a fight and so on, but I'm all for holding back."

"For what?"

"I don't know," Battles answered. "It's just a hunch I've got. We'd sure better find Verd first, if he's still alive. Might be we'll have to rope and tie him. He may be crazy as a loon. Anyhow, you don't just ride in and tackle an outfit that's got twenty men without giving it some thought and doing a little planning."

"We've got to find Verd, all right," Bruce said. "After that we try the law again. If we can get that fence down legally, we've . . ."

"You're wasting your wind," Battles said impatiently. "You ain't gonna hold me back waiting for the damned law that's had years to straighten this out. You won't hold Harper and McQueen and the rest of the JB boys back, neither."

Bruce didn't argue. He knew Battles was right. It had gone too far to wait for the law that apparently didn't care what happened in this almost forgotten corner of Grant County, yet it seemed to him the only reasonable course to follow. He was still thinking about it when they reached the rim above Rainbow. Bruce heard Battles mutter an oath; he saw him pull up and point into the valley.

The Rainbow buildings were a long way from the rim. They looked almost like a toy ranch, but even at this distance Bruce could make out the buggy that had stopped in front of the house. He saw a man get down and help a woman out of the buggy. The woman was Mary, and, as far away as he was, he could not mistake the tall, straight-backed figure of Morgan Drew.

"What do you know about that," Battles said softly. "The good Lord has delivered the enemy into our hands."

CHAPTER
NINETEEN

Bruce was not at all sure the good Lord had delivered Morgan Drew into his and Cole Battles's hands. As the two men threaded their way down the narrow, twisting trail that led to the floor of the valley, the conviction grew in Bruce that something strange and unpredictable had happened that had brought Mary and Morgan to Rainbow.

They reached the meadow at the base of the trail. Mary and Morgan were still inside the house. Bruce said: "Cole, this ain't the time to take Morgan."

Battles stared at him in astonishment. "What the hell? He's here, ain't he? There's one of him and two of us. We'll never get a better chance."

"We don't know why he's here," Bruce said. "Or why Mary's here. Let's find out before we jump him."

Battles stared straight ahead, his jaw set at a hard angle. Then he suddenly turned his head to look at Bruce, his face lighting up as if an explanation of Bruce's attitude had just occurred to him. "Oh, you mean you don't know where your pa will stand when it comes to a showdown."

"That's part of it," Bruce said. "It just doesn't make good sense for Morgan and Mary to be here. I want to know why before we start the ball."

Battles shrugged. "Well, I guess this is your ranch and it's your pa and sister, so I guess that makes it your ball."

They were silent until they reached the house and dismounted. Just as Bruce stepped down, Mary ran to him and threw herself into his arms. He had a brief glimpse off her face; he saw that she was crying and her eyes were red.

Bruce let the reins drag and held her in his arms, remembering that when she was a little girl she had loved him very much. When a bee stung her or she ran a splinter into a bare foot or when she fell down and hurt herself, she went to him to be comforted if he was closer than their mother. But it had been a long time since she had done anything like that, and he had no idea why she had done it now or even why she was crying.

He stood there under the noon-high sun holding Mary in his arms, her tears making the front of his shirt wet. He knew that Battles was standing beside him, stiff and sullen, his gaze on Morgan Drew, whose big body almost filled the doorway. Morgan's eyes were fixed on Battles, his right hand close to the butt of his gun.

That was the way it stood for what seemed a long time to Bruce, the hatred that Battles and Morgan Drew felt for each other almost a tangible thing poisoning the very air around them, then Mary pulled her head from Bruce's chest and swallowed.

"Pa's dead," Mary whispered. "The Indians murdered him. Morgan thinks it's what was left of the band that attacked us the morning we went to the fort."

Bruce had half expected this to happen, his father as stubborn as he had always been, insisting on returning to Rainbow alone and staying here where it was easy for anyone to murder him. It would have been a different story if he had gone to either the Big D or the JB, where he would have been safe, or if he had stayed at the fort, but Sam Holt had never been a man who took the easy or the safe way. He followed the course he laid out for himself and nothing could change him.

Still, knowing this, Bruce was hit hard by what Mary said. Knowing what could happen had not in the least prepared him for it. Several seconds passed before he could say: "Tell me about it."

"We don't know much except that he's dead," she said. "Morgan came over yesterday to get some of my things. I went to the Big D from the fort, so I didn't have anything with me except the clothes I had on and the few things I'd rolled up and tied behind my saddle. Morgan got here late yesterday afternoon. He found Pa's body by the corral gate. He'd been shot up close in the chest, Morgan said, so he figures they were waiting for Pa to come out of the house, probably early in the morning."

Bruce knew it could have been exactly that way. The Paiutes who had made the dawn attack had been severely punished. If they were still here, it would have been only natural for them to strike back at the ranch where they had been beaten off and several of the band killed. Bruce had no reason to doubt Mary's story as he looked over her head at Morgan who had stepped out of the doorway and now moved slowly toward them.

"That's right," Morgan said. "I didn't see any smoke from the chimney or anything moving when I rode up yesterday. I had a hunch something was wrong because it was about the time he'd be cooking supper. I hollered, but nobody answered, so I started looking around. When I was sure he wasn't in the house, I went to the corral. He was lying up close to the gate. His saddle horse was gone. I reckon that was all they wanted."

Mary took Bruce's hand. "Come and look at him. Morgan says we have to bury him today. He's got to go back to the Big D, and I won't stay here after what's happened."

"Go ahead," Battles said. "I'll take care of the horses."

Bruce turned toward the house, Mary still holding his hand. Morgan, walking beside them, said: "I carried the body into the house and laid him on the bed, then I shut the door and rode back to the Big D and told Mary. I'm glad you showed up, Bruce. It would be a sad thing to have buried him without you being here."

Bruce followed Mary across the front room into his father's bedroom. He stood at the side of the bed, staring at the square, stubborn face of the dead man who did not look at all like his father. He told himself that this was the manner of death. It had been the same with his mother and with Jason Bell.

164

"We didn't know you'd be here," Morgan said, "so Mary and I thought we'd bury him ourselves. She said he'd want to lie beside your mother. I decided not to bring the crew over for the service. There's a lot of work to be done on account of us being gone to the fort and all. Besides, I didn't want to leave the ranch unprotected with this renegade band still around. I don't suppose there's a preacher in a hundred miles of here, so we'll have to take care of it."

"No, there's not much chance of finding a preacher," Bruce said, thinking that Morgan had good reason not to ask anyone to come from the JB.

"It doesn't make any difference, does it, Bruce?" Mary asked. "I mean, not having a preacher? I can read from the Bible. We don't have a coffin, either, but Morgan said we'd roll him in the big piece of canvas that's in the storeroom. He said he'd see that a marker is put up."

"No, it doesn't make any difference," Bruce said dully. "We'd better start."

Turning, he strode quickly from the house. Battles waited outside for him. Bruce said: "We're going to bury him today."

Battles gripped his arm. "You believe that yarn, about the Paiutes murdering him?"

Bruce walked toward the barn, Battles falling into step beside him. Bruce didn't say anything for a time. He had a queer, detached feeling about this, as if he were standing apart from all normal life and activity and watching four people engage in this meaningless ritual that followed death. He shook his head and told himself that he would not lose contact with reality the way Verd Tucker had.

"I don't know, Cole," Bruce said as he opened the barn door. "It could have happened like Morgan says. You said yourself that no one could be sure whether all the Indians had left Steens Mountain."

"Yeah, I said it," Battles grumbled. "I guess I'd suspect Drew of killing his own mother if it would make him a nickel."

"We don't know for sure what happened and chances are we never will," Bruce said, "but we'll bury Pa, and Mary will read over the grave, and she'll go away with Morgan when it's finished. We will not do anything about Morgan today, Cole. Remember that."

"I know, I know," Battles said. "It would be disrespectful of the dead."

Bruce picked up two shovels and a mattock and left the barn, Battles still pacing beside him. They crossed the meadow to the fenced plot where Bruce's mother was buried. They started to dig, the ground so dry and hard that Bruce realized at once the task would take most of the afternoon.

Presently Morgan left the house, carrying Sam Holt's body in his arms. It was wrapped in the canvas Mary had mentioned. She walked beside him to the side of the grave and stood there as Morgan laid the body on the ground. She was holding her mother's Bible, which was so worn that some of the leaves were loose. Bruce stopped digging for a moment and leaned on the shovel, sweat pouring down his face.

Bruce considered saying something about the Bible, which his mother had read every night before she went to bed, but which had not been opened since she had died. Maybe he should read it once in a while, he thought, but there was no point in talking about it now.

Morgan took the shovel from Bruce and began working at the opposite end of the grave from Battles. After that it went faster, with Bruce using the mattock at one end and then the other. Late in the afternoon the grave was finished and the body was gently lowered into it.

The men stood motionlessly beside the grave, their heads bare, while Mary read the Twenty-Third Psalm and the Lord's Prayer, then she closed the Bible and tipped her head back to stare at the sky, which at that moment was a deep, unstained blue.

"God, our father was a good man," Mary said. "I guess we didn't know how good till after he was gone. Please take him to live in heaven with You and Jesus."

She began to cry and, turning, ran back to the house. Morgan stayed to help fill in the grave, then, as they walked back across the meadow, he said: "I'll hook up my buggy. Mary's going with me."

Bruce opened his mouth to say she wasn't going anywhere with Morgan Drew, then he remembered what he had told Battles, and what he had said to Harper about Mary's being of age. He went into the house, calling: "Mary!"

"Here," she said. "I'm in my bedroom."

He found her packing a suitcase with clothes. He said: "Mary, this is your home. Stay here and keep house for me. Half of Rainbow is yours."

"I know," she said without turning around. "We'll settle it later. You can buy me out. I can't stay here."

"Why not?"

"I'd be afraid," she answered. "Besides, Morgan loves me and he needs me. I'm going to keep house for him and Ben Louderman."

She went on packing her suitcase. Bruce stood in the doorway, feeling as if he had swallowed a cold stone that had lodged far down in his belly. She was bound to throw her life away on Morgan Drew; she would end up by being kicked off the Big D and she would probably kill herself, but there was nothing Bruce could do to stop her. If he forced a fight with Morgan and killed him, she would leave Rainbow anyway.

"You're sure you know what you're doing?" Bruce asked.

"I'm sure," she said, glancing at him, and then continuing with her packing.

He turned and walked back across the front room to the porch and stood beside Battles while Morgan drove the buggy to the door. A moment later Mary came out of the house, carrying her suitcase. She put it down and kissed Bruce on the cheek.

"I left some things I'll come back for," she said. "When you want to settle up on the property, come and see me. You know where I'll be."

He nodded. "Tell Morgan not to bother with the marker. I'll take care of it."

She picked up her suitcase, carried it to the buggy, and laid it behind the seat. Morgan remained in the buggy, holding the lines and making no effort to help her. She stepped up beside him, waved at Bruce, who raised a hand in farewell, then Morgan spoke to the team, and the buggy wheeled away, Mary's shoulder pressed against Morgan's.

"My God," Battles said. "Couldn't you stop her?"

"No, I couldn't stop her," Bruce answered.

He stood there, watching the buggy until it disappeared from sight. He had never felt so helpless in his life as he did at that moment, or so miserable.

CHAPTER
TWENTY

Bruce built a fire in the kitchen range. Battles remained outside, perhaps sensing that Bruce wanted to be alone for a while. Bruce put the coffee pot on the stove and sliced ham and started it frying, then he walked through the empty house, his footsteps making weird, echoing sounds. His mother had died in this house, his father had been murdered less than fifty yards from the front door, and now Mary had left for a life that could bring her nothing but unhappiness.

For a time he stood in the middle of his father's bedroom, looking at his parents' wedding picture in the ornate gilt frame. His mother had been a pretty young woman before hard work had taken its toll, but his father had changed very little, the broad, square face holding the same stubborn expression Bruce had seen so many times.

Here in this room were his father's clothes, his revolver, his tally book, a cowhide trunk in the corner that still held some of Bruce's mother's things. Sam Holt had possessed a sentimental streak that had not seemed to go with the rest of him. Now that he was dead, Bruce knew Mary had been right when she'd said at the graveside that Sam Holt had been a better man than they had realized when he was alive.

Bruce returned to the kitchen and finished making supper, thinking that what was past was past and nothing could be done about it now. Grieving accomplished nothing. Rainbow belonged to him. Mary had walked off and left it, so he saw no reason that he should settle up with her for a share she had obviously not wanted.

The trouble was Rainbow was too much ranch for one man. At the moment Bruce didn't know where he'd look for a cowhand. What was more, the job would be a dangerous one as long as Morgan Drew was alive. All the local buckaroos knew that.

Bruce called Battles into the house. They sat down and ate, neither saying anything for a time. Bruce lighted a lamp and cleaned up the dishes, turning an idea over in his mind. He and Cole Battles had been friends for a long time, but the events of the last few days had brought them closer together than before.

They went outside and sat on the porch in the twilight, pools of night blackness forming at the base of the cliffs that surrounded the valley, the rims straight, dark lines set against a slowly darkening sky. They smoked for a while, Bruce still thinking about the idea that had occurred to him a few minutes before.

"You got anything on your place to hold you?" Bruce asked finally.

"Not much and that's a fact." Battles took his pipe out of his mouth and looked at Bruce in the thin light. "A shack, a shirt tail full of cows, and a poor hayfield.

171

I've skinned a living out o' that quarter section I settled on, but damned if I know how. I've eaten jack rabbits till my ears started growing, and I've gone down to the lakes and shot ducks and et 'em till I've got webs between my toes and I wake up in the night going quack, quack. I'm just a dreamer, I guess, hoping that someday the fence will come down and I can get me a good ranch down there at the foot of Steens Mountain with a creek I can irrigate from."

"Like Verd with Skull Springs," Bruce said.

"That's right," Battles agreed. "Looks like we're both dreamers."

"How about throwing in with me?" Bruce asked.

Battles put his pipe back into his mouth, but it had gone cold, so he took it out again. The silence ribboned out for several seconds, then he asked: "What kind of a deal have you got in mind?"

"I hadn't thought it out exactly," Bruce said. "It doesn't look like Mary will ever live here again. Hard to tell how soon Karen will want to get married, now that I'm alone and Jason's dead. She might not even want to come here. Fact is, I wouldn't bring her to Rainbow now. Too dangerous as long as Morgan's alive. I guess that's one reason I wanted you with me."

"It's a good reason," Battles said. "The kind of reason that makes me want to come."

"Pa left some cash money," Bruce said. "I'd pay you regular buckaroo's wages. You could fetch your cattle over here. There's plenty of grass on the mountain during the summer, and I think we can put up enough hay to get both herds through a normal winter."

172

"Sounds good," Battles said. "You've got a deal. I've lived alone so long on nothing but hopes that I'd like to take a whack at trying to be human again. The Daniels boys have their mother and Rawlins is a hermit by nature, seems like, but I've had enough. If this business about Verd hadn't come up, I'd have left the country."

"We look for Verd first and then fetch your cattle over?" Bruce asked.

"That's the way we've got to play it," Battles agreed. "I've got a hunch that if we don't find him *pronto*, he's a goner."

"He might have run into that band of Paiutes," Bruce said.

"There ain't a Paiute within fifty miles of here," Battles said harshly. "Drew murdered your pa. You might just as well face it."

"Not yet." Bruce knocked his pipe out against his boot heel. "I don't give Morgan credit for having much good in him, but shooting down a man in cold blood who had done as much for him as Pa had is more'n even Morgan could do."

"Jason Bell was his friend and had been for years," Battles argued. "Any way you look at it, Drew killed Jason whether he pulled the trigger or not."

"It isn't quite the same," Bruce said. "Pa brought Morgan here. He was Morgan's father's best friend. When old man Drew died, Pa looked out for Morgan. Even after we settled here, Pa acted like Morgan was more of a son than I was. No, I don't think he could do it. No man could."

"Bruce, you're overlooking one big fact," Battles said. "Morgan Drew ain't a man. Not a sane man anyhow. He's crazier'n Verd is. He's got to be."

Bruce rose and slipped the pipe into his pocket. He stood, staring at the south rim, which was almost lost against the dark sky. Funny, he thought. He had hated Morgan Drew as long as he had known him, but now the thought of his actually murdering Sam Holt was so horrible and distasteful that he could not accept it.

"I hope you're wrong, Cole," he said at last. "Morgan's got enough to settle for without that."

Bruce went into the house and lighted a lantern. He told Battles to go to bed in Mary's room whenever he was sleepy. Bruce picked up the lantern and crossed the yard to the barn, wondering if he or Battles should stay up just on the chance Morgan had been telling the truth and a band of Indians was still in the country. He decided against suggesting it, mostly because he knew what Battles would say.

Stacked in the rear stall of the barn was a pile of boards that Sam had saved out of the last load of lumber he had hauled from the sawmill above the fort. Most of it was odds and ends that were too short to be of much use. Bruce hunted through them until he found a piece that would do. When he returned to the house, Battles had gone to bed.

Bruce sat up until midnight, carving his father's name and the dates of his birth and his death. He had done the same for his mother when she died. Sometime he would see that a proper stone marker was put up over both graves, but this would do for now. He thought about Mary and decided it wouldn't make any difference to her whether a stone was ever put up.

Bruce was so tired he couldn't think coherently, but he kept working until the carving was completed. In spite of himself and the knowledge that he had to accept what had happened, grief still made in his throat a lump that he could not swallow. Sam Holt had been a relatively young man who should have had many good years of life ahead of him.

Even after Bruce had finished the marker and gone to bed, he lay awake a long time, thinking of the injustice of life and death, and how there could be no peace for him and Karen so long as Morgan Drew and the Big D lay next to Rainbow.

Bruce woke before the sun was up. He built a fire, then carried the marker to his father's grave and shoved it into the loose dirt. He stood there in the cool morning air and stared at the sky, which was beginning to take on the gold and scarlet banners of the sunrise.

He wondered how it was after a man died. Was Sam Holt aware of what had happened? Was he looking down on this tiny, peaceful valley that had been his home for eight years and had held all his dreams of the future?

Quickly Bruce turned and strode back to the house. He was not one to give way to that kind of morbid thinking. For a time he was tempted to ride to the JB just to see Karen, then he dismissed the thought. Battles was right. They had to find Verd. It might be too late now.

He woke Battles and finished making breakfast. After they had eaten, Bruce cleaned up the dishes while Battles saddled the horses. He put as much food into two flour sacks as he judged could conveniently be tied behind the saddles, then left the house, a new thought startling him.

"Cole, do you reckon Verd is so loco he won't let us find him?" Bruce asked as he handed one of the sacks to Battles. "You suppose he might think we want to take him back to the hospital?"

"I've wondered about that," Battles said as he lashed the sack into place. "I don't know, but we've got to try to find him." He mounted and looked thoughtfully at Bruce. "Suppose we can't find him. Like you say, he might stay out of our way. Or he might be dead. What do we do then?"

Bruce stepped up, taking one last look at the house and barn and corral. He thought again of the injustice of his father's death, of how Sam Holt had seen this valley from the rim eight years ago and by some strange, intuitive knowledge recognized it as the place he was seeking, then he put these thoughts out of his mind.

"I don't know for sure what we'll do," Bruce said as he turned toward the road that led to the rim, "but I think we'll make a call on Morgan."

"Suits me," Battles agreed, "only we'd better figure on it some. Two men could commit suicide that way as easy as any."

"I don't want to call for help from the JB," Bruce said. "They've got to decide when to make their move."

They climbed out of the valley, stopping several times to blow their horses, then turned south when they reached the rim. The search for Verd Tucker would probably take them from one end of the Big D range to the other. Even this search, Bruce thought grimly, might be a way to commit suicide.

CHAPTER
TWENTY-ONE

They hunted Verd for three days without success. They found the remains of what they thought had been his campfires; they found tracks that seemed to go nowhere and could not be followed for more than half a mile. Early in the afternoon of the third day they saw below them on the mountain a line of grim-faced, heavily armed men led by Ben Louderman.

"What do you make of 'em?" Battles asked.

"Might prove two things," Bruce said thoughtfully. "I'd say Verd was still alive and he's been making a nuisance of himself."

"That's the way I'd call it." Battles glanced at the long slope of the mountain that stretched for miles on one side, then at the gorge that made a steep-walled trench on the other, and he shook his head. "We're idiots, Bruce. This is too big a country to find Verd, especially if he decided he didn't want to be found."

"I've been feeling a little bit like an idiot, all right," Bruce agreed. "You know, there's been times these last three days when I felt that somebody was watching me."

178

"And laughing up his sleeve all the time." Battles nodded. "I know just how you feel. Well, if Verd don't want to be found, we might just as well quit hunting."

"Let's try one more day," Bruce said. "We don't know why he don't want us to find him. It's my guess he'll find us if he takes a notion that's what he wants to do."

"It might mean he's so crazy he's afraid of his best friends," Battles said, "or it might mean he's not crazy at all and he's trying to tell us to go home and let him alone. Could be he doesn't want us to get hurt. I've got a hunch that, if we ran into that Big D bunch we just seen, somebody would get hurt."

"Somebody would for a fact," Bruce said. "Well, let's keep moving."

In the middle of the afternoon they topped a ridge and saw a line cabin directly ahead of them. They pulled up, surprised. This was new country to both of them, so neither had known the cabin was here.

From the rocks above them a man called: "Hook the moon, both of you!"

They raised their hands, glanced at each other. They had finally stepped into it, Bruce thought, and there wasn't a thing they could do except sit here and see what happened. For what must have been more than a minute they didn't move. The man in the rocks remained silent, and presently Bruce's arms began to get tired.

"What do you want?" Bruce asked. "We can't keep our hands up all afternoon."

"I was hoping you'd make a try for your guns," the man said. "I'd like to shoot both of you. Keep 'em covered, Slim. Now you yahoos can put your hands down, but the first move either one of you makes that looks like it's in the direction of your guns will get you a slug."

Bruce lowered his arms and rested both hands on the saddle horn. He turned his head to look at the man who had been talking. The buckaroo sat on a rock, a revolver in his right hand. About five feet from him a rifle barrel showed between two boulders that were not more than three inches apart. Bruce couldn't see the second man and wasn't sure there was one.

"I don't savvy," Bruce said. "Why do you want to shoot us?"

"You're Verd Tucker's friends, ain't you?" the cowboy said. "That's enough."

Bruce didn't know the buckaroo's name, but he remembered seeing him when they were at the fort. He was young, not more than twenty or twenty-one, tall and gawky, and at this moment he was possessed by a smoldering fury that would take very little to fan into flames.

"We're Verd's friends," Bruce said. "I don't see that's a good reason to kill us. I wouldn't kill you because you were somebody's friend."

"You might if you'd gone through what me 'n' Slim did this morning," the cowboy said angrily. "I had to go outside just about sunup and I damned near got my head shot off. Tucker was in these rocks and he kept us pinned down on the floor for three hours. After that

180

first bullet went past my head, I jumped back inside and shut the door. I couldn't even get to the window to shoot back. Every time we thought he'd gone, he'd cut loose again."

"He's a crack shot," Bruce said. "If he'd aimed to drill you, he'd have done it. He was just scaring you."

"He sure done a hell of a good job if that was what he aimed to do," the buckaroo snapped. "I never will get my natural growth now. He just plain scared me so bad I'm stunted for life."

"How'd you know it was Tucker?" Battles asked.

"Who else would do a stinking trick like that?" the Big D man demanded. "We know he's somewhere on the mountain 'cause he's been seen. Ben's hunting him now with some of the crew. He shot up the big house one night and this is the second line cabin he's had his fun with. We're gonna hang him. If you find him, tell him. Of course if Ben runs into you, he may hang you in place of Tucker."

"You shouldn't scare us that way," Battles said. "You might stunt our growth."

"You'll be taller if Ben finds you," the cowboy said darkly. "Your neck will be longer. Now turn around and ride back the way you came. Watch 'em, Slim. Let 'em have it if they make a wrong move."

They wheeled their horses and rode back over the ridge. When they were out of sight, Bruce said: "I wonder who Slim was."

Battles laughed, a shaky sound that held little humor. "I wasn't half as afraid of Slim if there was a Slim as I was of that cowpoke who was talking to us. He was just sore enough to cut loose whether he had a good excuse or not."

"Looks like Verd is having plenty of fun," Bruce said. "No wonder Louderman is out hunting him."

An hour later they were directly above the Big D buildings. They reined up and sat their saddles a good five minutes, watching the scene below them. The main house was a two-story structure that Morgan had built the first year he and Louderman were partners. He had planted a row of Lombardy poplars that had grown until they screened the front of the house. The county road ran parallel to the poplars, and a willow-lined creek flowed on the east side of the road.

Behind the ranch house were a number of buildings that made the place resemble a small town — a bunkhouse, a cook shack, a huge barn, a number of sheds, and a vast maze of corrals. Two men were working with horses in one of the corrals, and presently a woman came out of the back door and took washing off a line that stretched along the north side of the house. Bruce was too far away to recognize her, but he was sure she was Mary. As far as he knew, she was the only woman on the Big D.

Without a word to Battles, Bruce turned his horse and rode north. Battles caught up with him, asking: "You figure to go home?"

"It's a long ride," Bruce said. "We'll stay out another night."

Just seeing Mary at this distance that cut her down to doll size had been enough to make Bruce sick. He blamed himself, and yet, no matter how he looked at it, he didn't know what he could have done to keep her from returning to the Big D with Morgan.

Under no conditions would Bruce have forced a fight the day his father was buried. The only way he could possibly have kept Mary from leaving Rainbow would have been to use force, to have locked her in her room or tied her hand and foot. Either would have been ridiculous. Besides, any such act would have brought on a fight with Morgan. Still, guilt was a heavy burden on his shoulders, partly because Long Tom Harper had said: *If she was my sister . . .*

"I'll get her off that damned ranch," Bruce said. "I don't know how, but I will."

"Sure you will," Battles said. "I've knowed it all the time."

That night they camped at a spring under some big junipers at the head of a narrow cañon that widened out at this point to form a small bowl covered by grass. Boulders taller than a man's head guarded the passage below them, so close together that a horse could barely squeeze between them.

They built a small fire and cooked supper, then sat beside it and smoked, the bitterness of failure honing Bruce's temper to a fine edge. Tomorrow they would go home. He would help Battles drive his cattle to Rainbow's summer range on the north slope of Steens Mountain.

In a few days they would start putting up hay, and all the time they would be working with their guns within reach because they would have no way of knowing what Morgan Drew would do or when he would do it.

What would the JB do? Karen wouldn't want war even to avenge her father's death, but Bruce doubted that she could stop it. Sooner or later Ben Louderman and his men would run Verd Tucker down and hang him, and right now it didn't look as if there was much he could do about that, either.

Bruce went to bed, knowing that he had to break out of this trap of uncertainty and helplessness. He had never felt this way before. There had to be a solution that made sense. He was aware of Battles coming to bed, and he dropped off to sleep with the thought that he'd have the answer in the morning, at least enough of an answer to work with.

He woke at dawn with a haunting feeling that he'd had a very real dream of someone coming up the cañon during the night. He glimpsed a man squatting beside the fire that should have been out hours ago. Battles, of course, and Bruce shut his eyes to go back to sleep when he realized that Battles was still stretched out beside him. He sat up, fully awake now, and saw that the man was Verd Tucker.

Bruce let out a whoop as he threw back his blanket. He got to his feet and lunged toward the fire, his hand out. Verd rose and turned as Battles woke up.

"Where the hell you been, Verd?" Bruce shouted as he shook Verd's hand and pounded him on the back. "We've been looking for you."

Battles was there then, shaking Verd's hand and repeating what Bruce had said. Verd grinned at them and shook his head. He said: "You boys are lucky to be alive. You've been within fifty yards of me twice the last three days, but . . . you couldn't see lightning if it was right in front of you. Then both of you go to sleep so all a Big D man had to do is to walk in and slit your throats."

"Yeah, I guess he could have," Bruce admitted as he threw more wood on the fire.

The morning light was still thin, but when he turned back, the flames leaped up to throw a red glare across Verd's face and he realized the man had changed. There was a kind of animal-like wildness about him that shocked Bruce. It was in Verd's eyes as they flashed from Bruce to Battles and back to Bruce.

He was thin-lipped and wary and hard, and it took Bruce a little while to figure out what had happened. Even then he wasn't quite sure because Verd had a look about him that Bruce couldn't fully explain, but he decided that being hunted as he was had left its mark upon him.

Verd scratched his stubble-covered cheek and stared at Bruce. He said: "You're just plain stupid careless. You need somebody to look after you." He scratched his cheek again, the wildness in his eyes growing. Then he demanded: "You get Drew yet?"

"No, we've been looking for you," Bruce answered.

"He murdered your pa," Verd said. "I figured you wouldn't know."

Bruce felt his stomach tighten against his spine. He said hoarsely: "We buried Pa before we started looking for you. Morgan claimed the Paiutes done it."

Verd made a wolfish growl. "He's a damn' liar. I was on the south rim. I was too far away to shoot him, but

I seen the whole thing. Your pa was working around the corral when Drew rode up. He got off his horse and palavered with your pa, then he pulled his gun and shot him without no warning. He toted the body into the house, and he rode off, leading your pa's horse."

"That's about the way I figured it happened," Battles said.

Bruce turned away. He picked up a piece of juniper and tossed it into the fire, then stood staring at the flames. He could not doubt what Verd had said. He guessed he had known it all along.

CHAPTER
TWENTY-TWO

Bruce turned slowly from the fire to face Battles. He said: "Cole, you were right from the first. You had Morgan pegged better'n I did. Now that I look back, I guess I've been about as blind as Pa and Mary were. I didn't think Morgan could do it."

"I told you he was crazy," Battles said. "A man would have to be crazy to do what he's done."

Verd had been staring at Bruce. Now he wheeled to face Battles, his eyes wilder than ever. "No, Drew ain't crazy. I'm the crazy one. The doc at the fort will tell you that. Only a crazy man wants to see justice done to anyone as low-down mean as Drew."

"We can go to the law now," Bruce said. "You can testify you saw Morgan shoot Pa. I'll start for Canon City today. The sheriff can't put us off any longer."

"You're a fool, Bruce!" Verd cried shrilly. "How far do you think my testimony would go in court? I seen what I seen and I told you the truth, but Drew's lawyers would get everything I said throwed out. They'd prove I was crazy and my testimony wouldn't be worth a damn."

"That's right," Battles said. "If anything's going to be done, we're the ones who've got to do it."

"I say let's get at it!" Verd cried in the same shrill tone. "Now!"

Battles ignored him. He said to Bruce: "I don't reckon that what Verd saw changes anything. We've known all the time that as long as Morgan was alive and ramrodding the Big D, we'd have no peace on this range. I'd like to be partners with you on Rainbow. We get along fine and we could make it the best two-man spread in Grant County, but you 'n' me both know we wouldn't last a week. We'd get the same medicine your pa got."

Verd shook Bruce's arm. "Saddle up. We'll ride down to the Big D. Today. This morning. Right now. We'll hang Drew to one of his poplar trees."

"No," Bruce said. "Verd, I told you that afternoon we met at your place that I wouldn't stand for a lynching. What's more, we'd be committing suicide if we rode into the Big D now. There's a way to do this if we can figure it out, but that's not it."

Verd recoiled from him as if he thought he'd be contaminated. "You're afraid," he said, his lips curling in distaste. "You're scared."

"I don't want to die if that's what you're saying," Bruce told him sharply. "I've got a lot to live for."

"There is a way," Battles said. "Karen's got the same reason you have to want Drew dead. We can throw in with the JB outfit and we'd have enough force to wipe the Big D off the map. They're bound to be along sooner or later."

Bruce shook his head. "I've thought of that a hundred times and I've turned my back on it the same

188

number of times. If they come, it's because they made up their minds to do it. It'd be their decision and we couldn't keep 'em from making it, but it'd be a bloody battle and Mary might get killed."

Battles threw up his hands. "I suppose we go back to Rainbow and put up hay and wait to get murdered."

"No, we've waited too long now." Bruce turned to Verd, who was standing ten feet from him and still staring at him as if he were some kind of bug that should be destroyed. "I know a way to get at Morgan if we're lucky, but we'll need Rick and the Daniels boys. Will you stay out of trouble while we're fetching 'em? Or do you want to go with us?"

"No, I'm staying right here," Verd said haughtily. "I've been staying out of trouble, all right. You're the ones who had better watch out."

"You'll be here when we get back?"

"Right here," Verd promised.

"Let's cook up a bait of breakfast," Bruce said, "and get started. If we're lucky and find 'em home, we can get back by dark."

Verd was staring into space, the wildness gone from his eyes. He said wistfully, "It'll be good to get the Ninety-Nine together." Suddenly he lunged at Bruce and gripped him by the shoulders. "We ain't gonna be just a talk-and-spit society like you said. We ain't just little boys playing with passwords and grips and stuff like that. We're gonna do a man's job."

"That's right, Verd," Bruce said. "We'll do a man's job."

Bruce and Battles rode out of the cañon an hour later, Verd promising again that he would stay all day where they left him. Both Bruce and Battles were troubled about him. When they were out of earshot, Bruce asked: "What's going to happen to him?"

"I dunno," Battles said, "but he may wind up getting himself killed. He's sane and he's not sane."

Bruce nodded. "That's the way I saw him. Once Morgan's dead, I don't know what Verd's got to live for. He never did tell us why he kept out of sight for three days and let us look for him, then he just walks into our camp."

"Maybe he didn't know himself," Battles said. "Seemed to me he wasn't rational part of the time."

Bruce nodded. "That's what worries me. I'm going to give the orders because I won't stand for a hanging. I'll give Morgan a fair chance and I'll kill him. I might as well be the first to try. Somebody's got to. If he's faster'n me, you can have a try at him."

"You're aiming to fight him?" Battles asked in astonishment.

"That's right," Bruce said. "You know any other way to keep it from being called murder?"

"No, but . . ."

"All right, then," Bruce interrupted. "Morgan knows we're gonna fight. We talked about it once and he said he'd pick the time and place. He was wrong. I'll pick it."

"Why do you need us?" Battles asked. "Why don't you just ride down there and call him out?"

"He wouldn't come," Bruce said. "I don't think he's a coward, but he's a careful man. He'd rather figure out a way to kill me and be safe. What you and the others have got to do is to keep Louderman and the crew off my back."

Battles thought about it a while, then he asked: "You know the layout, don't you?"

Bruce nodded. "I've been in the house and the bunkhouse. It's Verd that worries me. I'm not sure he'll take my orders or keep a bargain after he makes it."

"Well, we can't leave him out of it."

"I know we can't," Bruce said. "We'll have to see how he performs when we get back. I don't know whether we've done right to leave him or not. He may take a notion to ride down to the Big D and go after Morgan himself."

"He might," Battles agreed, "but we can't run herd on him the rest of his life. If he's bound to get himself killed, he'll just have to do it."

Still, Bruce could not shake the feeling of uneasiness that gripped him. A man as unstable as Verd might do anything, even to challenging Ben Louderman and his buckaroos.

Rick Rawlins was sitting in the scant shade of his shack when Bruce and Battles rode up. He welcomed them as if he hadn't seen them for a year and wanted to know how the Indian fighting had gone.

"Fine," Bruce said, and told him briefly why they had come.

"I'm your man," Rawlins said. "I had just about decided to drive my herd," he emphasized the word, "to

191

the fort and sell 'em for what I could get, and then pack up all my valuable belongings that would go into one flour sack and ride out of the country."

As he saddled up, he went on: "A man gets ornery living by himself when he don't see no future. Well, I ain't seen much future from the day I settled here. I've asked myself a thousand times why I've stayed. Same with you, Cole. Same with the Daniels boys. Bruce is the only one who'll ever make anything out of what he's got."

Rawlins tightened the cinch and stepped up. "Now if we can get that fence down . . ." He stopped, suddenly embarrassed. "Damn it, Bruce, I'm sorry about your pa. I hadn't heard."

"You couldn't have," Bruce said. "Now what about Missus Daniels?"

"She'll raise hell and prop it up with a chunk," Rawlins said. "She never has liked for us to ruin her boys. That's what she says we've done."

Rawlins was right. Mrs. Daniels cooked dinner for them, then she put her hands on her hips and faced the table as they ate. She said: "Bruce Holt, you ain't taking my boys on this raid you're talking about. We've put a lot of work into our place and we can make a living on it. The valley will develop and we aim to be right here when it does. There'll be towns. Sawmills. A railroad, in time. I don't want my boys killed by Morgan Drew and his cut-throats before they get a chance to live. To hell with the fence. It don't mean a thing to us."

"You're wasting your wind, Ma," Hank said. "We're going. This is what we talked about a long time ago.

192

'Way back before the Indian trouble. Pete and me can't back out."

"Don't forget what Drew done to me," Pete said. "I wouldn't miss this for all the steers in Harney Valley." He looked at Bruce, who sat across the table from him. "I'm the one to fight him. You didn't get his blacksnake on your back."

"It was my father he murdered," Bruce said. "You'll take the deal like I said or you don't go."

"Then I reckon I'll take it," Pete said.

Suddenly Mrs. Daniels began to cry. "What will happen to me if you boys get killed?" she wailed. "Now that your pa's dead, you're all I've got."

"We never really disobeyed you before, Ma," Hank said, "but we're going to now. I ain't sure from the way you treat us whether we're boys or men, but I know one thing. If we don't go with Bruce and Cole and Rick, we'll be boys the rest of our lives if we live to be ninety years old."

Hank rose and stalked out of the house. Pete followed him a moment later, both going to the corral and catching and saddling their horses. Mrs. Daniels wiped her eyes with her apron and glared at Bruce.

"You're the one, Bruce Holt!" she snapped. "You and Verd Tucker and your crazy Ninety-Nine! I've told the boys a hundred times, if I've told 'em once, that you'd be the death of 'em if they kept running around with you."

Bruce rose and kicked back his chair. "Thanks for the dinner, Missus Daniels. Now let me tell you something. Maybe I'll be the one who gets killed, not your boys. Karen Bell and I are going to get married if I'm still alive when this is over. Well, I want to be alive. I want to get married and have a family and be a part of this country the same as your boys do. My father wanted the same thing, but he didn't get to see the towns and the sawmills and the railroads because Morgan Drew murdered him."

He walked out of the house, boot heels cracking against the floor. He heard a faint: "I'm sorry, Bruce. I didn't know about you and Karen." He went on, not looking back. Battles and Rawlins followed him out of the house, and within ten minutes the five men were riding south.

When they reached the gate in the fence, Bruce unlocked it, and they rode through. He had barely closed it when a Big D buckaroo who was riding the fence came at them in a gallop.

"Get back, all of you but Holt!" the guard yelled. "He's the only one who has the boss's permission to trespass on Big D range!"

The guard pulled his horse to a dust-boiling stop and found himself looking into the muzzle of Bruce's .45. Bruce said: "Get off."

"You go to hell!" the buckaroo shouted. "When I tell the boss what you're doing, you'll never use this gate again."

"We won't need to because the fence is coming down," Bruce said. "Now you'd better get off the horse."

The guard stared at Bruce and swallowed and shook his head as if he couldn't believe what he saw. "You look like you'd kill me," he said.

"That's exactly what I'll do if you're not off that horse *pronto*."

The man cursed as he dismounted. "When I tell . . ."

"Hang your gun belt on the horn and start walking," Bruce ordered. "Pete, you can lead the horse. He needs exercise."

The cowboy obeyed and started trudging south on the county road in the direction of the Big D buildings. Pete laughed as they rode toward Steens Mountain. "I wish he'd made a wrong move, Bruce. He was one of 'em that watched Drew give me that beating."

When they had gone a mile, Bruce told Pete to let the horse go. They began climbing the north slope of Steens Mountain soon after, Bruce taking the lead. He watched for Ben Louderman and his men, but there was no sign of them.

The sun was down and the evening light was beginning to thin when Bruce led the way through the narrow passage between the boulders. He saw that the fire was out, that Verd's horse was grazing at the upper end of the grass-covered bowl, but he didn't see Verd until he heard Battles, who was directly behind him, gasp and let out a strangled curse.

Bruce turned in his saddle and saw Battles point at the biggest juniper tree in the cañon. Bruce looked in that direction and reined up, a chill raveling down his spine. There, hanging from a limb of the juniper, was Verd Tucker. From the color of his face and the grotesque angle of his head, Bruce knew he was dead and probably had been for several hours.

CHAPTER
TWENTY-THREE

For what seemed a long time the five sat frozen in their saddles, staring at Verd Tucker's swaying body. Now and then it turned a little, the limb creaking under his weight. Bruce heard one of the men behind him being sick.

"Let's get him down," Bruce said as he dismounted. "Cole, ride over and cut the rope."

Battles took his knife from his pocket and rode to the juniper. Bruce put his arms around the body and eased it to the ground when Battles slashed the rope. Bruce stood motionlessly as the other men dismounted and crowded around him. He had a terrifying feeling that he was losing his mental faculties, that even time was standing still.

"Give me a hand with him, Rick," Battles said. "We'll pack him over yonder and lay his saddle blanket over him, then we'll figure out what to do."

"Do?" Pete Daniels cried out as if he were a child who was finding life too much for him. "There's only one thing to do. We'll get on our horses and ride to the Big D and we'll kill that murdering bastard!"

"No," Bruce said. It took Pete's anguished words to bring him out of his trance. "Maybe it seems like we've waited too long, but we've got to wait a little longer. We don't want to wind up the way Verd did."

Both of the Daniels boys grumbled something about waiting was what had killed Verd, and even Rick Rawlins said: "Bruce, if you're gonna give the orders, we've got a right to know what you're thinking."

"You sure do," Bruce said. "Help Cole move the body. I'll build a fire and get supper. Hank, you and Pete take care of the horses. I might as well tell you right now that it's a pretty slim chance we're betting on. If any of you boys want out, this is the time to say so. I was figuring on six men, but now there's only five of us."

They did what they were told. None of them argued with Bruce, but he felt the sullen anger that possessed all of them, an anger that was probably augmented by a feeling of guilt for having waited so long. But this stemmed from the wisdom of hindsight, not foresight, and Bruce told himself they had done the best they could with the knowledge they had at the time. The point now was to be sure they made no more mistakes.

When they were done eating, Bruce picked up a stick and knelt by the fire. He said: "You've heard me say this before and I'll say it again. There will be no lynching regardless of what Morgan Drew did to Jason and my father and Verd. I guess Morgan figures he's big and powerful enough to do what he damned pleases, but we're not. We all aim to live in this country. Let's not fix it so we'll wind up outside the law."

"Agreed," Battles said, tight-lipped. "Go on."

"One more thing," Bruce said. "We will not drag Morgan out of his house and murder him, though it's probably something we can do. We aren't the law and I've given up trying to make the law handle Morgan. But we've got to kill him. As far as I'm concerned personally, I'd shoot him down the same as I would a dog that's gone bad. The trouble is that where the law in this county won't work for us, it sure as hell will work against us, so the only thing I know to do is to get him out of the house and make him fight me. If he gets me, one of you can pick up the fight."

They were silent then, the sullen anger still hanging over them like a black cloud. Finally Rawlins said: "I guess we'll agree to that, though it's more'n he deserves. You've always looked ahead better'n the rest of us have and it seems like you're doing it now. I've got just one question. What about Louderman?"

"We'll let him live unless he tries to fight," Bruce said. "Somebody's got to run the Big D. With Morgan out of the way, Louderman will be reasonable."

Again they were silent as they considered this, but apparently it made enough sense to them so that none objected. Bruce had expected an argument because he was sure that Ben Louderman and the men he had been leading were the ones who had lynched Verd. Battles knew this as well as Bruce did, but the question he raised was an entirely different one that surprised Bruce and probably surprised the others even more.

"I agreed to this once," Battles said, "but I wish now I hadn't. Bruce, did you ever face a man with the idea you were going to outdraw him and kill him?"

"No."

"Are you fast on the draw?"

"No, but Morgan isn't, either," Bruce answered. "It ought to be a fair fight. I don't think I'll scare as much as he will."

"I haven't told any of you this," Battles said. "I wanted your friendship and I figured I had to be like the rest of you, so I kept mum about what I used to be. I'd better tell you now. I'm a wanted man in New Mexico because I was hired as a gunslinger. I was young, but I had a fast draw. I signed on with a big outfit for fighting wages because it was the quickest way I knew to make a stake. The trouble was, I killed the wrong man and I got out of the territory one jump ahead of a posse. I was on the run till I landed here. Let me take him, Bruce. I won't get killed. You might. You've got Karen to think of. I don't have nobody."

"Thanks, but it's my job," Bruce said. "I can't duck it. You know that as well as I do. Mary's my sister, Sam Holt was my father, and, if Jason Bell had lived a few more days, he would have been my father-in-law. I don't see any sense in blaming myself for not getting rid of Morgan sooner. It just never seemed like the time had come, but it's come now, and I aim to face it."

"All right," Battles said. "What's the plan?"

"I haven't thought of anything that's very smart," Bruce said. "If any of you know of a better idea, let's have it. I guess I'm the only one who knows the layout. I've been in the house and the bunkhouse. It strikes me that, with Morgan being as sure of himself as he always is, he might not have a guard out and he'd never think

199

of locking the house. He may have a man out watching for the JB bunch, but I'm betting he'll overlook us. That's why I think my scheme will work."

He made several marks in the dirt with the stick, then pointed to one. "Here's the creek on this side of the road. There's enough willows along the bank to hide the horses. If we ride out of here about two, we ought to reach the creek by four. It'll still be dark or close to it. All of them should still be asleep. I figure there's a good chance that half the crew will be out on the range somewhere. Even if that's the way we find it, we still might run into as many as eight men in the bunkhouse."

Bruce pointed to a second line in the dirt that paralleled the first one. "This is the county road that runs in front of the row of poplars. We cross it and go around the house to this shed. The bunkhouse is right beside it. We go from the shed to the bunkhouse. It's got a kind of lobby in front. The bunks are in a big room in the back. Right here is the touchy part of the whole scheme. If we do any shooting, we'll wake Morgan and Louderman and we'll have a fight on our hands, which isn't what we want."

"Morgan will use Mary to blackmail you," Battles said. "You thought of that?"

"I've thought of it," Bruce said. "Damn it, I've done nothing but think since the day we buried Pa. I kept telling myself there had to be a better way than what I thought of, but I haven't come up with it."

"There's a lot of luck to this," Battles said, "but it could work."

200

"Part of it depends on getting the jump on the Big D boys before they know what's going on," Bruce said. "Rick, Hank, and Pete will stay with the crew and keep 'em quiet. Cole and me will go into the house. It'll be fairly light by that time and Morgan or Louderman might be up, building the fire. Or Mary. Cole will hold the lid on inside the house and we'll get Morgan outside. I'll be there, too."

"We can do it," Rawlins said. "Let's be sure that fence comes down afterward."

"It will," Bruce said. "Now let's roll in. There's about half a moon later on before morning, so riding down the mountain won't be too slow."

Later, when Bruce was on his back with his head on his saddle and his blanket pulled over him, he found he could not sleep. He stared at the stars and considered what was ahead. He tried to think of everything that might go wrong and what they could do to counteract the bad luck that could whip them before they entered the ranch house. Once they got that far, Bruce felt certain they could go on to the end.

He could not put Mary out of his mind. For a little while on the day they had buried their father Mary was her old self, a sister who loved him as she had when they were children. He thought dismally that he would give anything to bring those days back when Mary had worshipped him because he was an older brother who was strong and was not afraid and could do anything she asked. Now it was different, and Bruce was as sure as he could be sure of anything that, if he shot and killed Morgan Drew, Mary would never forgive him.

He saw the moon tip up over the east rim and he knew it was time to go. He woke the others, though he wasn't certain that any of them had been asleep. A few minutes later they were mounted and riding down the mountain. Bruce was in front, and Rawlins, bringing up the rear, led Verd's horse, the body lashed across the saddle.

Bruce's estimate of time was almost perfect. They reached the creek close to 4:00 A.M. and tied their horses in the willows on the east bank. They waded the stream, which flowed over a gravel bottom at this point and was not much more than ankle-deep, then broke through the willows on the west bank, and raced across the road toward the poplars.

There was more light than Bruce had counted on. The moon was directly overhead, and the stars were glittering with fiendish brilliance. There was not the slightest trace of a cloud covering. Dawn was showing above Steens Mountain, and as Bruce, still holding the lead, skirted the ranch house and ran toward the shed that was close to the bunkhouse, he realized that if anyone in the house was awake and looking out of a window, they could be seen almost as distinctly as if it were broad daylight.

They reached the shed and stopped to catch their breath. A few seconds later the bunkhouse door opened and a man stepped through it, a lighted lantern in his hand. Bruce, watching from the shed door, saw that it was old Johnny Prebble, a former buckaroo who was too bunged up to ride and now did chores around the ranch.

Prebble was probably going to the cook shack to chop the day's supply of wood, Bruce thought. Bruce was surprised to see Prebble stop in front of the shed and put his lantern on the ground. A moment later Bruce saw another man coming from the barn. "Why ain't you out here watching for trespassers like the boss said?" Prebble asked.

"I've been in the barn with that mare, Judy," the second man said. "I thought I heard somebody running just now. That you?"

"Me, run with my rheumatism?" Prebble laughed. "You're a fool, Blackie, but your hearing is purty good. I heard it, too, but I ain't seen nobody."

The second man reached Prebble. From the blackness of the shed where he was standing, Bruce recognized the man who had just come up as Blackie Adams, a buckaroo who had worked for Louderman when Morgan had bought in with him. Now it seemed to Bruce that a rush of fear that was close to panic took possession of both of them as they glanced around with the uneasiness of men who knew they might be standing within seconds of a violent death.

"I told Ben he oughta have put more'n one man out for guards," Prebble said in a quivery voice. "I says after we stretched Tucker's neck, we could look for trouble from his friends, but he says the only trouble we'll have is with Sundown McQueen and his JB boys. He's got Munro watching for 'em."

Bruce estimated the distance between the shed door and the two men, telling himself that this was the bad luck he'd been afraid of. But it had not been all bad luck. At least they had reached the darkness of the shed before Prebble and Blackie had appeared.

"Wake all of 'em that are in the bunkhouse," Blackie Adams said. "I'll get Ben up. We'd better take a good look around here. I'm damn' sure I heard somebody running a while ago."

Turning, the Big D buckaroo started toward the ranch house.

CHAPTER
TWENTY-FOUR

Bruce knew they couldn't wait. They would lose the element of surprise if these two men woke everyone on the ranch, and surprise was the only factor they had in their favor. All Bruce could hope for was that Battles had the same thought he did.

"Now," Bruce whispered to Battles. "I'll take Blackie."

They left the shed in a lunging run. Adams and Prebble had their backs to them, so neither man knew what was happening until it was too late. Adams looked around just before Bruce hit him, Bruce's outflung arms catching the Big D man around the waist and bringing him down in a bone-jarring fall that knocked the wind out of him.

Adams tried to yell a warning, but the noise he made was no more than a gasping grunt. That was the last sound of any kind that he made for a while. Bruce pulled his gun and chopped him over the head with the barrel. He was knocked cold.

Bruce rose and holstered his gun. When he looked in the direction of the bunkhouse, he saw that Battles had taken care of Prebble in much the same manner. Bruce picked up Adams's feet and dragged him into the shed. He said to Rawlins: "Bring in the lantern, Rick."

Somehow in the tussle with Prebble, Battles had knocked the lantern out of his hand. It was on the ground, still lighted. By the time Rawlins was back in the shed with it, Bruce and Battles had the unconscious men in the rear of the shed.

"You done good," Pete Daniels said, laughing softly. "I thought for a minute or two the fat was in the fire."

"It damned near was," Bruce said. "Gag him, Cole. You boys look around for some rope."

They gagged the Big D men with their own bandannas. Pete Daniels found enough rope to tie both men, then Bruce blew out the lantern. He said: "We lost some time I didn't figure on."

Bruce ran out of the shed, his revolver in his hand. For the first time he was scared. He thought he'd figured out the time down to the minute, believing that everyone on the ranch would be sleeping the soundest at this hour.

He had thought, too, that he and his friends would need the early dawn light to avoid the fumbling and hesitation that was bound to come from feeling their way in the night darkness. Now Bruce knew it would be close, that they could not afford the loss of any more time.

Bruce slowed up when he went through the front door of the bunkhouse; he eased across the first room, the others following in single file. When he reached the door opening into the room that held the bunks, he lunged through it, yelling: "On your feet! Get your hands up! We're Verd Tucker's friends!"

The Big D men woke up as suddenly as if a bolt of lightning had flashed the full length of the bunkhouse, one of them moving in such a hurry that he lost his balance and hit the floor with a thud that sounded like that of a dropped sack of wheat. Another fumbled for his gun. Bruce, seeing what he was doing, grabbed him by the shoulder and whirled him around and clouted him on the side of the head with his gun barrel, sending him reeling. Whatever fight there was in the rest of them disappeared when they found themselves facing five men with cocked guns in their hands.

In the pale light that fell through the windows, the Big D crew was a bedraggled bunch, six of them, their hands in the air, still groggy from sleep, their hair disheveled, all in their underwear and two with their shirt tails flapping.

"Outside," Bruce ordered. "Cole, lead 'em out of here. Line 'em in the yard. You boys better know we found Verd. You'd lie if we asked you who was in on his hanging, but I've got a hunch you all were. If we knew for sure, we'd string up the bunch of you, so don't give us any excuse to shoot you."

They marched out of the bunkhouse without a word, Battles waiting outside for them. Pete chanted: "Right, left, right, left, pick 'em up and put 'em down." Then he began to laugh. He said: "Bruce, did you ever seen a tougher-looking bunch in your life?"

"I never did," Bruce said. "Get their guns. Find a sack and put 'em in it. Then come outside and help Hank and Rick."

Battles lined the prisoners up in front of the bunkhouse. A moment later Bruce joined him. He said to Rawlins and Hank Daniels: "Whatever you do, don't start watching me or Cole when we come out of the house with Morgan. If you get your eyes off this bunch, they'll scatter and we'll have our tails in one hell of a crack."

"We'll take care of this end," Rawlins said. "Better hurry. It's getting daylight."

Bruce wheeled and ran toward the back door of the ranch house, hoping that Ben Louderman or Morgan didn't wake up in time to see what was happening. If either man cut loose from the kitchen door with a rifle, the situation would be reversed in a matter of seconds.

Cole Battles caught up with Bruce before he reached the house. Bruce yanked the door open, both men slid inside, then crossed the kitchen to the front room. Ben Louderman came down the stairs, yawning and running his hand through his thinning hair. He didn't see either Bruce or Battles in the dim light until Bruce said: "Hoist 'em, Ben."

Louderman was still two steps above the floor when Bruce gave him the order. His head jerked up, he stumbled and almost fell before he recovered his balance. He stood paralyzed, his right hand poised over the butt of his gun.

"What do you want?" Louderman asked in a quavering voice.

Bruce strode toward him, calling back to Battles: "Light a lamp, Cole!" When he was ten feet from Louderman, Bruce said: "I hear Verd Tucker swiped your revolver while you were sleeping at the fort. You have to buy a new one?"

"He had it on him," Louderman snarled. "The damned sneak thief."

"He had it on him when?" Bruce asked.

A match flared to life behind Bruce. Battles touched the flame to the wick of a lamp on the claw-footed stand in the middle of the room, and replaced the chimney. In the improved light Bruce saw Louderman's face turn gray. He apparently realized he had been trapped.

Then, perhaps because he saw no hope for himself, he blurted: "When we strung him up, damn it! He was still carrying my iron."

"How'd you find him?" Bruce demanded.

"He found us!" Louderman snapped. "He was in the mouth of that cañon where he'd been holed up. When we rode below him, he cut loose. He killed a couple of my men before one of my boys worked behind him and got the drop on him."

Bruce wasn't surprised. He had been reasonably sure that, if Verd had remained in the cañon as he had promised, Louderman and his crew would have gone past without finding him because the mouth of the cañon had been hidden by brush. On the other hand, the result might have been the same because Louderman certainly knew the cañon was there since it was on Big D range. In any case, Bruce did not question his story. It would have been like Verd to challenge Louderman's party, perhaps not caring whether he lived or died.

"So you hung him," Battles said, coming up to stand beside Bruce. "You got any good excuse to go on living?"

"I ain't no outlaw!" Louderman snapped. "Tucker was."

"The hell he was!" Battles said passionately. "You've got a lot of gall to talk about Verd being an outlaw after what Morgan Drew's been doing. You're as guilty . . ."

Battles subsided when Bruce made a sharp motion with his left hand. He said: "Ben, Morgan's the one we're after. Which room is he in?"

Louderman hesitated, his gaze on Battles for a good ten seconds before he looked at Bruce. He asked: "Can I count on that? Is Morgan the one you're really after?"

"That's what I said."

Louderman moistened his lips. "The front room upstairs on the left."

Bruce climbed the stairs as silently as he could, but it seemed to him that every step squealed a shrill warning before he reached the hall. He wondered which room Mary occupied. He wondered, too, why she wasn't up and cooking breakfast.

The hallway was carpeted, muting his footsteps as he moved quickly toward the room Louderman had indicated. He stood motionlessly for a few seconds, listening outside the door. Morgan was whistling cheerfully as if he were very satisfied with himself this morning.

210

Bruce put his hand on the knob, turned it, and, slamming it so hard that it banged against the wall, he went into the room, moving fast. Morgan stood in front of the mirror combing his hair. Now he wheeled, but he made no motion toward his gun.

"Well, Bruce, this is an unexpected pleasure," Morgan said pleasantly. "I didn't know you were calling."

"This ain't a friendly call," Bruce said. "We're going downstairs and out into the backyard. You said once that we'd settle our differences someday, and you'd pick the time and place. I don't think I'd like the place, Morg. You'd be hiding behind a rock and I'd get it in the back like Jason did, so I'm picking the time and place. Now. Behind your house where your crew can see what's happening."

"Oh, I don't think we'll do it this morning," Morgan said, still smiling pleasantly. "I'm not quite ready, and I don't care for the place, either. Maybe another time and place would be better."

If Morgan Drew had the slightest worry about what was going to happen, he didn't show it. He was as handsome and confident as ever, a fact that irritated Bruce. Knowing the man as he did, it shouldn't have bothered him, but he couldn't help it. This was the way it had been for the eight years Bruce had known him. Regardless of the situation, Morgan had the capacity to face life with the same smiling confidence he showed now.

Bruce moved on into the bedroom, motioning with his left hand. "Out," he said. "Down the stairs and through the kitchen. Cole Battles has his gun on Louderman, two of your men are gagged and tied in a shed, and three of my friends are holding the rest of your buckaroos in front of the bunkhouse. For once you're going to face the man you're trying to kill and you know I'll be ready. I guess Jason and Pa didn't know what you were going to do, did they?"

Still Morgan didn't move and the irritating smile grew with the passing seconds. Then he said with evident relish: "You didn't figure this thing out, son. Mary, keep him covered while I relieve him of his iron."

Bruce turned his head just far enough to see that Mary was standing in the doorway, a pistol in her hand that was aimed at him. No, he hadn't figured it out. Not quite. Morgan was right again.

CHAPTER
TWENTY-FIVE

Bruce's first thought was that if Mary fired, she'd hit him. She was a good shot with a revolver, and at this distance she couldn't very well miss if she really made an effort to shoot him. His second thought was less of a certainty. He decided it was an even bet whether she would fire or not. Even if she loved Morgan and hated him, the old bonds might be strong enough to keep her from actually pulling the trigger.

Morgan took a step toward Bruce and stopped when Bruce said: "That's far enough, Morg. I'm not sure whether Mary's going to shoot me, but you can be damned sure I'll shoot you if you keep coming."

"Let him have it, Mary!" Morgan shouted. "What are you waiting on?"

"He murdered Pa, Mary." Bruce sidled toward her, still watching Morgan. "It wasn't the Indians like he told us. That's why I'm here. We could have taken him outside and hung him just like they hung Verd Tucker yesterday, but I'm giving him a chance at a fair fight. That's better'n he did for Pa or Jason Bell."

"He's lying!" Morgan's voice was shrill, his confidence gone. "Damn it, shoot him!"

"Verd saw him murder Pa, Mary," Bruce said, still sidling toward her. "I guess that's why they strung him up. To keep his mouth shut. You can ask Cole Battles. He heard what Verd said."

"I tell you he's lying!" Morgan's voice was almost a scream. "I don't want to fight him. Shoot him while you can."

She looked from Bruce to Morgan and back to Bruce, her face ghastly pale. Doubt was in her, enough doubt so that in this final moment she could not bring herself to pull the trigger. Bruce reached out, twisted the revolver from her fingers, and backed into the room again.

"You'd better move, Morg," Bruce said. "You've got more of a choice than you gave Pa. Either go down the stairs and out into the backyard, where I'll give you a chance for your gun, or you'll take it here in the belly. You've got three seconds to make up your mind. I've had all the stalling I can stand."

Morgan didn't take the three seconds. He picked up his clean, stiff-brimmed Stetson and clapped it on his head. He strode to the door and stopped to glare at Mary, who had retreated into the hall.

She stood with one hand raised to her throat, tears filling her eyes. She was wearing a maroon robe over her nightgown, her hair had not been combed, so she must, Bruce thought, have got out of bed just before she came to Morgan's door with the revolver.

"He's my brother, Morgan," Mary whispered. "I . . . I couldn't shoot him."

214

"You're a stupid fool!" Morgan said harshly. "You had a chance to save us both."

He went down the stairs, Bruce close behind. He heard Mary sobbing in the hall above him. For just an instant he felt a hint of sympathy for Morgan. In this one final moment of testing, Morgan's control over Mary was not so complete as he must have been confident that it was.

When they reached the front room, Morgan paused to glance at Louderman, who had backed away from Battles and stood against the far wall. Morgan said: "What a bunch of idiots I was depending on. I thought you put some guards out."

"I did," Louderman said defensively. "I had Blackie out here and I sent Munro down the road to watch for the JB bunch. I dunno how these fellows . . ."

Morgan didn't wait to hear what Louderman had to say. He went on into the kitchen and through the door into the backyard. He looked at the crew, his lips curling in disgust. The Big D men were standing in front of the Daniels boys and Rick Rawlins, their hands in the air. It was a ludicrous scene, the erstwhile tough cowhands clad only in their underwear, except for the two whose shirt tails dropped well down on their drawers.

Morgan stopped and sucked in a long breath. "By God, if that ain't a sight."

Bruce had the feeling Morgan was working for time, and then the thought came to him that possibly the rest of the crew that was somewhere out on the Big D range might be riding in early this morning, that Morgan had made plans for a raid of some kind, perhaps on the JB.

"Move," Bruce ordered. "Over there to the left."

Bruce was dropping back in the other direction, wanting to put some distance between them. He saw that Mary had come to the kitchen door and was watching, a hand still clutching her throat. Suddenly the need to get this over with was a driving urgency in him.

"All right, Morg!" Bruce called. "That's far enough! Make your play!"

Morgan turned to face him. The man's aplomb was gone; he had the desperate expression of one who was looking squarely at the ugly face of death. He moistened his lips, he threw a glance at Mary, and suddenly it seemed to Bruce that this was only a shell of the Morgan Drew who had lived all these years behind the poised and confident exterior that Mary and Sam Holt and everyone else had seen. Then the thought came to Bruce that Morgan had always been a shell, a bluffer, a master of pretense, and a cold-blooded murderer.

Now Morgan Drew was caught between turning and running away and losing forever the reputation he had built that had never had the slightest foundation in fact, or moving forward to face Bruce's avenging gun. He must have known that, if he ran away and lived, he could not stay here; he could never face his partner or his crew or even Mary. But Morgan Drew was impelled to run, so he ran toward Bruce.

216

Morgan lifted his gun from leather and fired, a wild shot that was a foot or more over Bruce's head. It must have come to him that this was crazy, that he was throwing away whatever chance he had. He stopped suddenly and stood, spraddle-legged, and brought his gun up again.

Bruce had made his draw when Morgan fired. Now he leveled his gun and squeezed off a shot, the bullet rocking Morgan back on his heels. Morgan pulled the trigger, a convulsive shot that kicked up the dust at Bruce's feet.

Bruce strode forward, watching Morgan, who struggled to stay upright, to lift his gun again, but he lacked the strength to do any more than raise it halfway. His control seemed to fail all at once and he went down, his clean, stiff-brimmed Stetson falling off his head into the gray dust of the yard.

With the last of his great strength, Morgan brought himself up to his knees. Blood gushed out of his mouth and flowed down his chin. He said thickly: "I had to kill Sam. He wouldn't sell to me."

Then Morgan pitched forward on his face. Two shots thundered from inside the house just as Mary ran out of the kitchen. She sat down in the dust and lifted Morgan's head to her lap, then looked up at Bruce. She said: "I hate you! God, how I hate you!"

He was going to ask her to come home with him, to tell her again that Rainbow was her home, but now, seeing the expression on her face, he realized there was no use. He had known it all the time, and he had said it, and yet the hope had lingered that she might change at the last minute. At least she had not shot him in Morgan's room when she'd had a chance. Perhaps it was the last good memory he would have of her.

He wheeled away from her and strode toward the Big D buckaroos, only then remembering the dream in which Mary had cried out for Morgan to shoot him. It hadn't been quite that way, and yet there wasn't much real difference. Mary was the only blood relative he had, and she would never return to Rainbow.

"We'll leave your guns across the creek where our horses are," Bruce told the Big D men. "Come and get 'em after we're gone, but if you make any wrong moves before we're out of here, we'll turn around and come back and we'll wipe the Big D off the map. And another thing. The fence is coming down. Don't try to put it back."

He jerked his head at Rawlins and the Daniels boys, and they strode rapidly toward the horses. Battles joined them as they circled the house. He said: "Louderman made the mistake of trying for his gun."

Bruce said nothing. He was sure he would never know the full truth as to why Louderman made that mistake, but he was certain Battles had not intended leaving the Big D without squaring up for Verd Tucker.

They reached their horses, mounted, and rode downstream for fifty yards before they forded the creek and turned north on the county road. A rider passed them, keeping his horse in a hard run.

"That was Munro," Bruce said.

"Look." Battles pointed at the dust that was rising ahead of them. "The JB crew is making its move, but it's a mite late."

They pulled up when they met the JB men, Long Tom Harper and Sundown McQueen in front. "You're a little slow if you're aiming to do what I think you are," Bruce said. "Morgan and Ben Louderman are dead."

That jolted them, and Harper said sharply: "Why didn't you wait? You knew we'd be along. We were held up because Karen insisted on burying Jason fit and proper. It took a little time to get a preacher up here from Winnemucca."

"They lynched Verd Tucker." Bruce motioned toward his body. "Morgan murdered Pa. We waited too long the way it was."

"That's a fact," McQueen conceded. "Jason was like your pa, I guess. He never could see through Morgan Drew. Not till right there at the last."

Harper looked at him indignantly. "I suppose you did."

"No, I reckon I didn't," McQueen admitted. "Well, we'll go on and put the fear of God into the rest of the boys who're there."

"The fence is coming down," Bruce said, thinking this was the time to meet the issue head on.

"So Karen told us," McQueen drawled, "but I'll tell you boys one thing. It don't mean we're letting everybody move in on the JB and steal our range."

"We sent word about the funeral, but there wasn't anyone home," Harper said. "Karen's at Rainbow now. She's waiting for you."

"Thanks," Bruce said, and rode on past the long line of JB riders.

When they reached the rim above Rainbow, Bruce said: "I'll come over to Verd's place later today. I reckon you'll bury him beside Sue."

Battles nodded. "I figured that was the thing to do. We'll wait."

Bruce rode down the steep trail to the floor of the valley. Karen must have been watching for him. She left the house and ran toward him the instant he came into view. He put his horse into a gallop, and was out of the saddle when he reached her and on the ground before the sorrel had come to a complete stop.

Karen threw herself into his arms, she kissed him with the wild abandon of a woman who had not seen her man for years. When at last she drew her head back, he saw that tears were running down her face.

"Oh, come on, now," he said. "This is a happy day."

"It *is* a happy day," she said. "It's so happy I'm . . . I'm crying."

He looked at her full red lips, the nose that was a little on the pug side, the freckles that swept from the outer edge of one cheek across to the other, and at her brown eyes. He thought of the proud way she walked, her shoulders back, her firm, young breasts thrust forward, and suddenly he felt a lump in his own throat when he remembered there had been times these last few days when he had not thought he would be alive to hold her in his arms again.

"I love you, Karen," he said. "There's no reason to wait any longer."

"No reason at all." She wiped her eyes and smiled a little. "Bruce, I'll come here to live. Long Tom's going to stay in the JB ranch house and take it easy and run things like Father did, and Sundown's going to stay on as foreman. The main thing is that Rainbow and the JB will act like neighbors."

In the back of his mind this had been the big problem. Rainbow was his and he wanted to stay here, but he had been afraid that Karen would want him to run the JB. "That's the way I'd like it," he said. "Now about the date?"

"I got the preacher to stay after the funeral," she said, "but he can't stay long. He has to get back to Winnemucca."

"Why now," Bruce said in a grand manner, "we can't put the preacher out, but on the other hand we don't want to rush into a thing like this, so maybe we'd better wait a while. Say, till tomorrow?"

She laughed. "It's funny, Bruce. That's exactly the day I told him."

About The Author

Wayne D. Overholser won three Spur Awards from the Western Writers of America and has a long list of fine Western titles to his credit. He was born in Pomeroy, Washington, and attended the University of Montana, University of Oregon, and the University of Southern California before becoming a public schoolteacher and principal in various Oregon communities. He began writing for Western pulp magazines in 1936 and within a couple of years was a regular contributor to Street & Smith's *Western Story Magazine* and Fiction House's *Lariat Story Magazine*. *Buckaroo's Code* (1947) was his first Western novel and remains one of his best. In the 1950s and 1960s, having retired from academic work to concentrate on writing, he would publish as many as four books a year under his own name or a pseudonym, most prominently as Joseph Wayne. *The Violent Land* (1954), *The Lone Deputy* (1957), *The Bitter Night* (1961), and *Riders of the Sundowns* (1997) are among the finest of the Overholser titles. *The Sweet and Bitter Land* (1950), *Bunch Grass* (1955), and *Land of Promises* (1962) are among the best Joseph Wayne titles, and *Law Man* (1953) is a most rewarding novel under the Lee Leighton pseudonym. Overholser's Western novels, whatever the byline, are based on a solid knowledge of the history and customs of the

19th Century West, particularly when set in his two favorite western states, Oregon and Colorado. Many of his novels are first-person narratives, a technique that tends to bring an added dimension of vividness to the frontier experiences of his narrators and frequently, as in *Cast a Long Shadow* (1957), the female characters one encounters are among the most memorable. He wrote his numerous novels with a consistent skill and an uncommon sensitivity to the depths of human character. Almost invariably, his stories weave a spell of their own with their scenes and images of social and economic forces often in conflict and the diverse ways of life and personalities that made the American western frontier so unique a time and place in human history. *Fighting Man* will be his next Five Star Western.

ISIS publish a wide range of books in large print, from fiction to biography. Any suggestions for books you would like to see in large print or audio are always welcome. Please send to the Editorial Department at:

ISIS Publishing Limited
7 Centremead
Osney Mead
Oxford OX2 0ES

A full list of titles is available free of charge from:

Ulverscroft Large Print Books Limited

(UK)
The Green
Bradgate Road, Anstey
Leicester LE7 7FU
Tel: (0116) 236 4325

(Australia)
P.O. Box 314
St Leonards
NSW 1590
Tel: (02) 9436 2622

(USA)
P.O. Box 1230
West Seneca
N.Y. 14224-1230
Tel: (716) 674 4270

(Canada)
P.O. Box 80038
Burlington
Ontario L7L 6B1
Tel: (905) 637 8734

(New Zealand)
P.O. Box 456
Feilding
Tel: (06) 323 6828

Details of ISIS complete and unabridged audio books are also available from these offices. Alternatively, contact your local library for details of their collection of ISIS large print and unabridged audio books.